---- ★ ----

As she sat on the rocks above the beach putting her sneakers back on, Amy felt that tingle alerting her again, telling her she was almost remembering something. She sat motionless looking at her footprints in the wet sand. Footprints. Handprints. Fingerprints. Foot, hand, finger, thumb. What else had she seen Wednesday morning when the sliding sawdust revealed a shoulder, then an ear and a cheek, then an arm and a hand, when the body had been exposed in the mill shed?

Amy had told Dort she had a feeling she knew something she didn't know she knew. What was there about that scene in the Morse Mill sawdust shed that felt familiar, that hung on the edges of her mind?

---- ★ ----

A. CARMAN CLARK

THE
MAINE
MULCH
MURDER

W⊕RLDWIDE.

TORONTO • NEW YORK • LONDON
AMSTERDAM • PARIS • SYDNEY • HAMBURG
STOCKHOLM • ATHENS • TOKYO • MILAN
MADRID • WARSAW • BUDAPEST • AUCKLAND

To Robert Hugh Barron
—who believed in me

THE MAINE MULCH MURDER

A Worldwide Mystery/February 2004

First published by The Larcom Press.

ISBN 0-373-26483-6

Printed in U.S.A.

Acknowledgments

I owe thanks to the librarians and book shop owners who grew tired of my complaints at not finding the kind of small-town mystery I wanted to read and told me to go home and write one. And then kept asking how my book was progressing.

I'm grateful to members of the Maine State Police Homicide Division and court officials who gave their time to speak to writers' groups and answer questions on the steps of procedure in Maine when a body is found.

Many thanks to the members of Maine Media Women who listened to page readings and expressed their opinions when I needed help in creating scenes others could visualize. My friends Karen Van Allsburg and Annie Stanforth offered objective suggestions on my use of language and transitions whenever I asked and Arnold Webster, arborist, answered my questions on hemlock cones.

I'm particularly grateful to my children, who encouraged me to keep going off to Granton and welcomed me back to Sennebec Hill.

ONE

AMY CREIGHTON discovered the body while gathering sawdust to mulch her strawberry bed. Another person might have screamed or turned at once to run out of the shadowy lumber-company shed; but Amy's immediate reaction followed the pattern of control she had trained herself to use when faced with unpleasant or shocking situations. She took a deep breath and let it out slowly. She had just filled the hatchback with the seventh bag of sawdust and returned to the shed to collect her scoop. "Fidgits," she said, and then, "Double fidgits," as she looked down into the face of a young man, a face and body the sliding sawdust now revealed.

Stomach spasms and rapid breathing belied her calm exterior as she steadied herself. Amy had seen death many times in her sixty years, but this death was not a natural, nor an expected, final passage. No one on the verge of becoming an adult should be cold and lifeless. And how had he come to die here, under heaps of sawdust in this mill shed?

Voices and truck motors were audible beyond the fifty-foot patch of alders, willows, and brier bushes that separated the two-story sawdust shed from the office of Morse Mill and Lumber Supply, where the nearest phone was. After standing still and taking deep breaths to ease the spasms in her stomach, Amy retraced her path to the wide step that ran along the open front of the shed. She turned to view the scene.

Morning sunlight from high windows on the east side showed cobwebs across the culvert-sized pipe through which sawdust from the mill was blown into the storage shed. Had it been one day or several days since the blower had been used? Spiders spin quickly.

The body lay just beyond the center of the shed floor, just where blown sawdust would cover it first. Several willow shrubs that had grown higher than the sills on the far side of the front of the building were bent and broken. Something or someone had moved into the shed from that point, instead of up the wide step by the drive-way, the step Amy used. She looked at the wilted leaf buds with a gardener's eye—those branches had been broken recently. On the weathered floorboards in front of her, her path from the step to the center of the shed showed in the thinly spread sawdust. She found it easier to scoop her bags full from the high piles. Less bending; less lifting.

Amy had carried sawdust out of this shed for years. The three-sided, two-story building stood only a stone's throw from the mill office and about the same distance back from the country road, but the shadowy, echoing shell had always seemed isolated and lonely. The thick tangles of weed shrubs that softened sounds from the mill yard also served as a visual screen.

Without crossing beyond the wide entry step, Amy took another look at the young man before she turned back into the cool sunshine of the May morning. She catalogued his jacket as L. L. Bean's, new, and his haircut as recent. Eyes closed. Hadn't she read or been told that someone closes the eyes of a dead person—

keeping the spirit in or spirits out? Or was that an old wive's tale?

The mill yard hummed with activity. Amy backed her compact in between two trucks and headed for the office. Blinded momentarily by sunlight reflecting off the office windows, she would have bumped into the man coming down the steps if he hadn't reached out to hold her shoulders.

"Amy Creighton. What brings you out of your gardens on a fine May morning?"

Amy ignored the question. "Dort, where's your truck? Quickly. I need to tell you something."

The genial smile shifted to a questioning look but Dort Adams stepped down to the driveway, cupped his hand under Amy's elbow, and guided her over to and into his brown pickup. "Yes?" His bushy eyebrows went up with the tone of his voice.

Amy waited until he was settled behind the wheel before she said, "I just found a body. A dead body."

"Where?"

"Over there. In the sawdust shed. I scooped and the pile slid and there he was."

"He?"

"A young man. Not local. You're a constable. Whom do you call—the sheriff?"

Dort was already dialing the car phone. Discordant thoughts flipped and flopped and crisscrossed in Amy's mind. She was glad she hadn't had to use the mill office telephone and surprised that Dort's shabby old truck had a phone. How long had Dortemus Adams been town constable? When had ol' down-to-earth Dort moved into the new era and put a phone in his battered pickup? Amy had planned to mulch her strawberries that morning, before the black flies hatched out in full force. Now, she would have to wait for the sheriff. And try to keep her stomach from churning. Try to deal with the questions tumbling in her head.

"Are you OK?"

Dort had put the phone back on its holder and was looking down at her. Even while sitting Dort looked down on others. His height was due to a long torso as well as long legs and, gradually, over fifty-eight years, this frame had been padded to a solid 220 pounds. Dort Adams was the largest constable in the county. Few folks argued with him in village matters pertaining to those of the sheriff's department. Behind his back, townspeople called him the "gentle giant."

Amy brought her mind back to the present activities in the lumber yard and practiced her habit of calm control. "Certainly I'm OK. I was just head-wandering."

"Sheriff's on his way. Medical examiner will be along. I'd like to have a look before they get here. You want to sit in my truck or your car?"

"Neither. I want to see your reactions. Hear what you notice that I missed. Find out if you recognize the poor boy."

Dort pursed his lower lip as though cutting off words he might have spoken, then smiled and started the truck. " 'Don't argue with Amy.' I heard that the week I started school in this town and folks are still saying it. The boys in my class told me your father treated you the way other fathers treated their sons. Told me he argued with you to give you practice. Right?"

Amy responded with a half smile. "Dad's favorite line was 'God gave you brains and he expects you to use them.' Better pull over and park in Ira's drive although I've probably messed up any tire tracks that might have been in that road to the shed."

Dort pulled into the curving drive of the small brown house opposite the entrance to the yawning sawdust shed. They looked over at the open side of the weathered storage building, looked at each other, and then opened the doors of the truck. The rutted driveway to the sawdust shed was still damp with dew and Amy's tire tracks were fresh and clear. As she followed him along the grassy edge, she thought of a beagle setting off on a hunt.

"Did you notice signs that anyone had been gathering sawdust before you? Signs of shoveling after the blower had been shut off?"

"I didn't think of that," Amy answered. "I did notice the pile was high. That makes it easier for me."

Dort stopped on the wide step. Amy moved up beside him. Just off center, beyond the support beam, the face and shoulder of the body were clearly visible. A blond head with the chin tipped down like he was resting. No blood or bruises could be seen.

"How many bags did you fill before you uncovered the body? Were you using a shovel?"

Amy's eyes moved from the body to the broken bushes and her voice sounded distracted and hesitant when she answered, "I use a plastic dustpan as a scoop. No shovel. My hatchback holds seven full bags. I didn't uncover the boy. It just happened. You know how dry sawdust slides, runs. Like sand on dunes. I looked down and saw the sawdust had shifted, and there was the face. At first glance, I thought I knew him. But I don't. Do you? Is he anyone you know?"

Before Dort could answer, Amy pointed at the willow shrubs. "Those are bent and broken."

"I see."

They stood in silence, looking from the broken

branches to the body. The clean pine scent of the sawdust mingled with damp earth smells as the morning sun warmed the open area in front of the shed. Dort Adams rubbed his left ear with his index finger. Amy Creighton tapped her collarbone with the fingers of her right hand. Neither noticed the unconscious motions they had seen each other make for half a century.

Amy had been a seventh grader when the Adams family moved to Granton and their large, quiet son entered fifth grade. Being a new kid in a country school demanded a certain amount of adjustment. Being a new kid with the name Dortemus added to that adjustment. After the fights stopped, someone commented that when Dort Adams rubbed his left ear, he was thinking. And it was best to stand back and let him think.

Amy Creighton was busy with her own thinking. Living willow shrubs don't break. In Maine in May, pussy willow branches are flexible, pliable, still dripping catkins—the fuzzy kind that look like caterpillars, the kind boys take to school to drop on girls' necks to make them squeal.

Once again Dort cupped Amy's elbow and steered her back along the edge of the driveway and across the road to the truck. Then as he paced the curved drive, he kept his eyes on the sawdust shed.

"When did Ira leave?"

"He went up last week." Amy looked at the house with every window shade pulled down. "Said he wanted to get in some fishing before the sports came."

"He didn't rent the place this year?" Dort was standing under one of the front windows that was directly opposite the drive to the sawdust shed.

"It's rented, but to college people. They can't come

until the end of the month. Nellie Small's feeding the cats until then. Does it on her way to work. Mornings.''

Amy watched Dort rub his ear again. She gave him a full minute for thinking before she said, "My mind is skittering. One part of my head is asking, What's the proper behavior when one has just discovered a dead body? But this boy is a stranger. So another part of my mind asks other questions. Why is a strange young man in the Morse Mill sawdust shed in Granton, Maine? Was he drunk, went to sleep, and suffocated in the sawdust? Or did someone put the body in there? I want to know what you're thinking.''

Amy's habit of thinking questions aloud annoyed some people, but Dort, coming back across the lawn, seemed to be amused. "I'm wondering the same things. We're nine miles down from Route One. There's no car." His expression changed and Amy caught a glimpse of sadness, a look she remembered seeing on that gray November day when she and Dort both left Granton, going their separate ways.

"An unattended death means an autopsy. The sheriff will be calling the state police." Before he could say more, the county sheriff's car pulled in and stopped behind Dort's truck. While the photographer assembled his gear, the medical examiner pulled in and parked his black car on the lawn. Amy watched the four men approach the shed, confer, and move inside.

Had she discovered an accident victim or a murder?

TWO

MURDER? AMY RAN this idea around in her head and came forth with, "We don't have murders in Granton, Maine." That line loosened facts stored in her mind, accumulations buried through the years. *What about Ed Hume? He killed his wife here in East Granton only seven years ago. Remember the reactions in the village when that woman from New Jersey poisoned Wilber Hackett? Didn't your own grandmother find a body in the brook behind your house?*

Amy watched the sheriff and his men talking in front of the mill shed. Watched the doctor, ankle-deep in sawdust, bending over the body. If it wasn't murder, what other explanation was there for a stranger lying dead over there? A hitchhiker might have decided to stop and rest, but why would he die? It wasn't logical for a boy wearing a new L. L. Bean jacket to be on this peninsula road, headed to or from Sacaja Harbor, without a vehicle.

She looked at her watch. Twenty minutes before noon. The discomfort in her stomach was probably hunger. She was also aware that the three cups of coffee she'd had before leaving home were causing another kind of discomfort.

Behind Ira's house, just above his tool shed, was the old outhouse. Amy smiled as she walked around to the back of the house and headed down the path. The sight of that small building, stained the same brown as the house, reminded her of the arguments Ira and Libby Bellhouse had had about "that old privy" after they put in a bathroom. They argued about it for years, publicly and privately. The neighbors took bets on who would win.

Ira wanted to tear down the outhouse, burn it, get it out of the space he claimed was right to build a dog run for his beagles. Libby allowed as how that convenience was handy in garden time—it was sturdy, nicely surrounded by healthy day lilies, and Ira's barking dogs could run on another part of their seven acres. Libby said her husband considered his beagles more important than her bladder. Libby Bellhouse didn't linger long after the doctors found she had cancer. Ira sold his hounds and took a summer job cooking in a sporting camp in northern Maine. Came back to Granton after hunting season. Last fall he put a new roof on the old outhouse.

Amy smiled again when she came out of the privy, back into the sunshine, and turned to fasten the outhouse door. The wrought iron hook, probably salvaged from an old barn, was set at her eye level, straight and even. Ira was a neat man. Some folks called him nasty neat. The door hook and the hinges had been oiled—recently. But the step before the outhouse door was askew. Only a bit. Amy might not have noticed if she hadn't been thinking of Ira's fussy, neat habits as she rehooked the door. She backed up for a better look.

The outhouse step, a thin rectangular piece from the quarry, about as big as an oven door, was slightly twisted. An inch or two of brown earth showed along the upper left-hand corner, raw soil not covered by the green, fast-growing grass.

"Sheriff believes there was foul play." Dort's voice startled her. He had come down across the back lawn and stood a few yards behind her. "Skull's broken on the right side, the side that was down, next to the floor. Body was there before sawdust was blown in. Morse says they ran the blower twice yesterday."

Amy forgot the crooked step as she looked up at Dort, who was frowning and gazing over her head at the wooded slope behind the outhouse. He wasn't seeing her and his gaze didn't appear focused on the woods. What was he seeing? Amy's mind replayed that startling picture—a smooth cheek showing up after her scoop set small rivers of sawdust running. Dry sawdust flowing down, disclosing a shoulder, an arm, an ear, a face, a hand.

"Do they know who he is?"

Dort continued staring but he answered, "No wallet. Probably about twenty-one. Not known to the sheriff, the doctor, or to Morse. He'll show the photo to men at the mill. See if anyone there knows the boy."

Amy watched Dort looking into the distance, another mannerism exhibited during their school years. His classmates used the expression "out-of-town" to describe Dort Adams's stance and far-off look when he distanced himself mentally to concentrate. Amy waited for his return.

"Mrs. Creighton?" The sheriff spoke from the corner of the house. Was he wondering why his local constable and Amy Creighton were standing together, without talking, in front of Ira Bellhouse's brown outhouse? The part of Amy that had never knuckled under to codes of proper behavior wanted to say, "We're flipping a coin to see who goes first."

Instead, she gave Dort's arm a quick squeeze, went

up the path and around to where the sheriff waited. In country language, Amy knew *about* the sheriff but she didn't *know* him. Sheriff Woodman's father had been a Boston police officer who liked to fish. One spring, on a fishing trip to Ward's Pond in East Granton, the Boston lawman had been caught by one of Lawry Tibbett's girls, angling for a husband so she could get out of town. Now their son, Bentley Woodman, had come back to live in Maine and be the county law officer.

They sat in the sheriff's car. Woodman had only a few questions. Yes, Amy told him, it was about nine a.m. when she left home. At the mill shed she filled seven bags and carried them to her car. After loading the seventh, she went back to get her scoop, saw sawdust shift, slide down to reveal the body. She hadn't moved or touched anything in the shed except the sawdust. No, she did not recognize the young man. Yes, she would be at home for the rest of the day.

As Amy walked back to her car, she nodded to people who had stopped to see what was going on. Some of those in the mill yard had come on business but cars now lined both sides of the road to Sacaja Harbor. An ambulance and a state police cruiser had arrived and parked near the sheriff's car. Everyone driving by could see that something had happened. Two state troopers began directing traffic but the flashing blue lights of their cruiser seemed to draw more curious folks to stop and look.

Emma Waldron and Martin Morse were standing on the top step outside the mill office door. Martin waved at Amy as she settled into her car. Martin was not a small man but he looked diminished there beside Emma. They were looking out over the weedy patch of alders and briers, watching the law officers outside the sawdust shed. Amy, who fumed at times because she had to use a step stool to put dishes up in the cupboard but liked being able to buy herself sweaters in the boys' department, wondered what it felt like to be bigger, always noticeably larger than classmates, neighbors, and family.

Amy remembered Emma in first grade, Emma Ramsdorff then, an awkward, unsmiling child, far larger than anyone else in her class, wandering alone on the school playground. Granton folks said the only time Emma looked happy was when she was talking about her house, the great old Gregg house she and her husband, Arthur Waldron, had been restoring for years. Together they had done a remarkable job, turning what had been an empty, neglected building, probably the oldest original house on the peninsula, into a showplace, visited by garden clubs and history enthusiasts.

Amy edged her compact out of the mill yard and drove home on automatic pilot, scarcely aware of the four miles of familiar winding roads. If the sawdust had been blown in yesterday, Tuesday, the boy must have died Monday night. She thought of him as a boy. Dort said he was about twenty-one. How did Dort judge? Amy had given up trying to guess ages. Thirteen-year-olds wore their parents' clothes. Girls slathered on mascara before their braces came off and, if you didn't know the family, who could tell a tired thirty-year-old from a fifty-year-old fitness advocate?

But why was that body in the sawdust shed? A multitude of thoughts and questions had come into Amy's mind since she first glimpsed the boy's cheek. The question she kept repeating was, "Why there?" Farm and village folks up and down the peninsula helped themselves to sawdust at Morse Mill. Farmers hauled truckloads for barn bedding, for lambing pens and henhouses.

Some gardeners collected sawdust in bags as she did, mostly in the spring, to cover paths or to keep down weeds in strawberry beds or raspberry rows. There were weeks when no one went near the place, when the blown-in sawdust piled up more than fifteen feet and ran down in rivulets, forming heaps on all sides. What Granton residents didn't know about the mill shed and the free sawdust?

When she stopped in her home driveway, her dog Chutney raced around the car, up the front steps, then back again as though Amy had been gone for weeks. But the dog responded to a firm "Stay!" command. Chutney exhibited intelligence and enthusiasm but lacked definitive canine characteristics. Her shaggy eyebrows suggested sheep dog ancestry. The sweeping tail had a collie look. But the large, rust-colored body was as sleek as a Chesapeake retriever. Three years ago, when Amy rescued her from the county animal shelter, the puppy's fur was splotchy, like an English spaniel that had rolled in mud. But when the small dog curled up in a basket by the stove, Amy thought its color resembled the rhubarb chutney she was stirring. The dog's coat soon changed in both texture and color, but the name stuck.

Chutney settled under the kitchen table with a dog biscuit while Amy ate a quick lunch. Then the dog asked to go back outside when Amy went down the hall to her office. She was still in that office, oblivious of time and weather, when Chutney's barking called her attention to a knocking at the front door.

A shaft of sunlight from the west shone through a rain shower. Dort Adams stood on her doorstep watching a double rainbow arched across the eastern sky. Neither of them spoke until the hall clock began to strike.

"Time to talk?" Dort asked.

Amy waved him inside. "I've been working. Publisher wants the edited copy mailed back on Friday. I had no idea it was so late. I didn't know it was raining. Coffee?"

The coffee was ready in a large thermos. Amy sliced a loaf of carrot yeast bread and brought butter and cream to the table. They sat at the old oak table beside a wall of new windows and watched the rainbow fade. The long rays of the setting sun spotlighted the wet pines beyond the garage. Amy's hand trembled as she lifted a slice of bread. Had it been more than thirty years since she and Dort Adams sat together at this table? Three decades since they had exchanged more than casual greetings when they met in the village?

"Bent asked me to talk to you. He wants to know what other people you see gathering sawdust at this season, more about who drives into that mill shed and who might notice a car or truck in that driveway." Dort looked at Amy over the rim of his coffee mug. "The boy was moved in there after he died."

"Monday night?"

"Probably. They'll do the autopsy in the morning."

Amy refilled their coffee mugs and cut two more slices of bread. Monday night. She spread soft butter with one of the silver butter knives Carrie Parker had given her last month when she visited the elderly woman down in Sacaja Harbor. Monday night there'd been a church supper at the harbor. With music.

"Monday night this week there would have been more cars than usual on Harbor Road. The Old Baptists had their fund raising. That group working to restore the old church at Coffin's Cove. I know—they aren't all old and not many of them are Baptists—but the newspaper report messed up the facts when they started that project. The name stuck. That's what the harbor folks call them. Monday night they had a public supper in the town hall. The Sacaja school put on a music program with children from the Granton school and I think some from the high school. There could have been ten or more cars coming back from the harbor after nine p.m.'' Amy watched Dort reach for another slice of bread. ''But would anyone driving by notice a car pulled in on that road to the shed?''

''Any music program kids live on that section of the harbor road? Near the mill?'' Dort closed his eyes as though trying to picture that section of town. ''The only house with a view of the mill or the sawdust shed is Ira's and you said he went upcountry last week.''

''The Norton children live this side of the mill,'' Amy said. ''If they were in the program, someone else did the transporting. That driver may have slowed down looking for the Norton driveway.''

''Bert Norton?''

''Bert and Doris.''

''Bert still drinking?''

''Both of them, I hear. But I don't know.'' Amy shifted in her chair. ''I don't want to repeat what I don't know to be true. When I drive on Harbor Road I often pick up the Norton children. There are three of them. They're polite, nice kids. But they never mention their parents in any way—good or bad. Why don't you call Eb Simmons? I think he arranged the music program. He'll be able to tell you who drove down from Granton Monday night and what time the cars came back.''

Dort held up the silver knife he had been using and rubbed his finger over the twisted handle. ''Family silver?''

"Not my family. Carrie Parker gave them to me. Set of six. Said my grandmother admired the design, the twists in the handles. You know, if you need information on anyone down at Sacaja Harbor, Carrie's the one to ask. She's not a gossip and she doesn't have a mean bone in her body, but Carrie Parker knows every skeleton that ever rattled on this peninsula: The girls who went west for a year to visit an aunt no one knew existed; the boys who suddenly left town to train with an uncle in Canada; why school children from different families sometimes look like twins. When you saw that dead boy this morning, did you have a feeling, however fleeting, that he had a familiar look?"

"Yes. So did Martin Morse. But it was, as you say, fleeting. I couldn't catch it again."

"What happens next?" Amy asked. "Fingerprints? Reports on missing persons? Checking for an unclaimed car? The boy was so healthy looking. Is it because I'm sixty that I keep thinking of him as a boy? You've also said 'boy.'"

"The sheriff's men and the Maine state police will check out the angles you've mentioned," Dort said. "My job is to find out if anyone here on the peninsula noticed a stranger over the weekend or on Monday, if anyone noticed a car or truck near that shed on Monday or Monday night. There'll be a request for information on radio and TV news tonight and in the morning. We know there are a few out-of-state fishermen here this week; can check names and addresses in license records. But in this part of Maine in the first week of May, we don't have many strangers. And Granton folks notice. Dennis Peabody claims his aunt knows the make and year of every car or truck driven by every person in this town."

"And the hour they pass her house," Amy added. "Poor Hattie. Her legs are so bad. She doesn't get out much. But her eyesight's still keen. She told me she wrote a thank you note to the governor when the highway crew put a stop sign at the end of Olde Road just beyond her lawn. Helps her watching."

They sat in comfortable silence, thinking of Hattie Howard. For years, town folks passing Hattie's house had slowed to wave at the figure beside the window. After the stop sign was set in, newcomers, delivery truck drivers, and fishermen responded to Hattie's waves. Bill Bean beeped the school bus horn each morning and afternoon and the children raised their hands in greetings. Once last winter, when Hattie wasn't at her window, the kids insisted that Bill stop the bus and find out what was wrong. Hattie was OK. She was on the phone. Her Chicago cousin had called in the morning instead of the evening to wish her a happy birthday.

"Remember Ben Howard?" Dort grinned. "Remember the time we put the mallard egg under his best setting hen?"

Amy nodded, then cocked her head to one side and asked, "Who else got some of those eggs? I remember bringing them up from the river, handing them up over the bank to you. What started that venture? Ben and Hattie thought it was funny. They named their duck Adam. But Will Waldron was not amused. I can still feel his anger. We didn't hurt anything or anyone but that man shook with rage."

"Will had a terrible temper. My father saw him smash a church window once. Will paid to have it replaced before the whole town found out. The mallard eggs were your idea. You asked me to help because you were afraid of broody hens. They pecked your fingers. What were we then, about fourteen?''

"I think I was fifteen, because that was the year my grandmother gave me a new bicycle. We wrapped the eggs in my sweater and carried them in the bike basket. You must have been thirteen.'' Amy stood up and crossed the room to answer the phone. "That was the summer we frightened the campers on Sacaja Pond with our ghost on a raft and our hoots echoing in the darkness.''

The phone was on the wall near the door to the front hall. Amy held it out to Dort. "It's Sheriff Woodman. For you.''

Dort's end of the conversation consisted mostly of grunts in negative tones. He hung up, picked up his hat, and headed out into the hall. But as he turned toward the front door, he looked back at Amy and said, "Thanks for the coffee. Good bread. There's a car with New York license plates parked behind Hank Gustaffson's boathouse. Sheriff wants me to check it out.''

THREE

THURSDAY DAWNED cold and gray. At six a.m. a light but steady rain was falling on lawns and gardens already well soaked during the night. The strawberries wouldn't be mulched this morning unless the weather changed.

Chutney went off on her morning patrols, scouting the pond shore to see if any camps were occupied, eliminating woodchucks and chasing squirrels. Amy switched on the lights and the electric heat in her office, closed the door and settled down to work.

After almost three hours, she took a break to stretch. Sitting at a desk was the negative part of editing. Amy's exercise bar was on the shallow porch, outside the door to the backyard. When Amy stopped to stretch, she stretched. She was hanging from the bar, counting to sixty, when Dort came down along the side of the house, tripped over the gutter drain and yelled, "What the hell are you doing?"

"Stretching. What are you doing here while I'm working?"

"You just said you were stretching."

"Oh, Dort. Don't niggle. I'm getting the kinks out after sitting for three hours and I have several more hours ahead of me." Amy pushed her toes down, stretching each leg, but continued to hang.

The big constable stood on the lawn looking at Amy

without his usual, detached, laid-back expression. "I'm sorry I yelled. But do you have any idea how you look hanging there? I phoned. Talked to your machine twice. I pounded on the front door. Then I come around the house and you're hanging there, motionless."

Dort looked and sounded both angry and confused. Not the easy going, gentle giant demeanor usually observed. She hadn't seen Dort Adams off balance since...not for years.

Amy hand-walked until she was above the step stool and let herself down. "I have to get back to work. What was it you wanted?"

"I came to talk, to hear your thinking on what we've learned since last night."

It was quarter past ten. If she lost her momentum now, the book wouldn't be ready to mail out tomorrow. She wanted to know what Dort had found last night. What the sheriff and state police knew this morning. But Amy was aware of her limitations. She knew how difficult it would be to regain her focus on the manuscript.

"Come back at one. Come for lunch. I have soup cooking in the Crockpot. I'd like to bounce some thoughts against someone, things I thought of after you left last night."

Amy went back to her desk but it wasn't easy to push aside the questions and images that had moved forward in her mind as soon as Dort appeared. What had they learned? Who were "they"? Had the owner of the New York car been located? *Concentrate, Amy. You said you'd express mail the book on Friday. That's tomorrow.*

The publisher called at noon as scheduled. Amy had four questions for him. He had a half-dozen for her. Their conversation, which Amy recorded, was business-like but had a friendly, informal tone. The two had never met. Amy had no idea whether Sam Mozeson was forty or sixty, fat, bald, or a health nut. When she talked with him, she pictured him with a neatly trimmed gray goatee, a professorial face. The résumé she'd sent when she applied for work with his firm had given her age but the publisher had no way of knowing whether, at sixty, she was short and fat, or tall, thin, and wrinkled. To Amy the important aspect of this business relationship was that they communicated with honesty. They respected the expertise each had and used. Distant colleagues.

That phrase had just crossed Amy's mind when Sam Mozeson said, "I hear you had a murder up there yesterday."

"How did you know?" Amy was startled. Her personal life in Maine was set apart from her editing work for a New York publisher, a dual identity she took for granted. How did Sam Mozeson know more than her mailing address and phone number?

"Maine state police called. The young man who was killed was wearing my son's jacket."

For twenty-four hours Amy's mind had been repeating, "Who is he? Why is he here?" So her immediate response was, "Then your son knows the boy, knows the name of the boy who was killed. Who is he? What was he doing in a mill shed on this peninsula?" Amy's voice rose to a tone and tempo Sam had never heard in eight years of telephone conversations.

"Amy, I don't know who the murder victim is. My son Tim drove up to Maine last Sunday. He's due back on Saturday. We've been on edge since that first call from Maine. We knew from the sheriff's description that our son wasn't the victim. But that's all we know. We don't know where Tim is staying or how to contact him."

"The jacket—bright colors, new. How did the sheriff know it belonged to your son?"

"Tim's name and address were written inside one pocket. When Sheriff Woodman called and said Granton, I told him I knew you. He told me you had discovered the body. I know your feelings about being interrupted during your working hours so I waited for this time of our scheduled contact. You're upset."

"Wrong word. I'm distraught." Amy took a deep breath and then another. "That boy was so young and healthy looking. It always bothers me when someone dies so young. And this was murder, which makes it worse. I'm trying not to let myself get rattled because then I won't be able to concentrate and the constable is coming at one." Why was she telling her New York publisher that Dort Adams was coming at one p.m.?

"Amy, may I call you this evening? I'm not cold and unfeeling. I'm in a state of shock. We're checking with Tim's friends. The Maine police are looking for his car. I'd like to talk with you later. By then you may know more and I hope we will."

"Thanks, Sam. I'm more upset than I realized." Amy's voice was back to its usual calm control but she added, "I keep thinking there's something I should remember, something I saw. Was your son planning to meet friends in Maine? In this part of Maine?"

"We don't know. Tim is thirty-two, recently divorced, between jobs, but involved in some museum consultation. He stopped in New York to leave his grandmother's silver with his mother and then drove to my place to see me. Told both of us he was headed up to Maine and would see us again when he came back on Saturday. That's all we know."

Amy asked, "Does he sail or fish? May is not the month to camp in Maine."

Sam's voice sounded tired. "I don't know. I don't know my son. I really don't know what he does or likes or thinks. But I want him safe."

"I'll talk with you this evening," Amy said. "By then we should both know more."

Sam Mozeson, publisher, the man whose company issued the checks that paid the bills, the wise and diplomatic editor, the man who chose to publish the kinds of books Amy enjoyed editing, had a wife and a thirty-two-year-old son. He and his wife didn't live together. He and his son were not close. And today that son, Tim Mozeson, was somewhere in Maine and the police wanted to talk with him.

As Amy cleared her desk and filed notes on their business conversation, she realized she had learned more about Sam Mozeson in the last half-hour than in eight years of telephone talks concerning manuscripts. Some time ago Sam had mentioned that he liked spicy Mexican food but had never spoken of a son.

The rain had stopped but heavy gray clouds hung over the valley. Aromas from the kitchen promised a hot and hearty lunch. Amy brought the Crockpot to the table and put the rest of the carrot bread loaf to warm in the microwave. She set out the orange pottery bowls, the ones her Camden friend made to fill Amy's request for bowls deep enough to keep soups hot. Then she went to look out the front door.

Dort was sitting in his truck, rubbing his left ear and studying a map. Amy called twice before he raised his head, shook off his concentration, and opened the truck door. The map dropped to the ground. "Sacaja Peninsula, the enlarged edition." The map showed every el-

evation, cove, and stream. Dort's muddy boots looked
as though he'd been wading through some of those
streams. Wading streams had been part of the exploring
Amy and Dort had done through their high school and
college years. Was that how this sheriff's constable had
spent the morning?

FOUR

THE NEW YORK CAR was registered to Hank Gustaffson's houseguest and Hank had not been pleased when their predinner rest was disturbed by law officers at the door.

"Law officers? Who was with you?"

"Two state police. Bent asked them to wait for me because I knew the territory. Knew Hank." Dort put his hat on the stool under the telephone and leaned against the doorframe. "Hank's guest this week is a tall blond. She came out wearing a red satin robe and an icy expression. Didn't say a word when she handed us her driver's license and car keys. Car was locked. City habit. But Hank's mood changed when we told him why we were checking all unfamiliar vehicles."

Hank had seen lights in a cottage on the other side of Sacaja Pond on Monday night. Said he thought it odd. It was earlier in the season than those Portland folks usually opened camp and they always went back on Sunday night. He hadn't noticed any lights over there since Monday but neither had he looked for them. Brought out his pond association list and gave us names and addresses of the camp owners.

"We hadn't had any reports of vandalism on that side of the pond," Dort said. "The smashing, boat bashing, and broken windows have been at the bigger summer places along the river and at Sacaja Harbor. State police have cooperated with the sheriff in checking these, so before we drove around the pond to check those camps we called in, reported the sighting of lights on Monday night and the information on camp owners.''

Dort told her that from the gravel road behind the three small buildings they could look across Sacaja Pond and see the lighted windows of Hank Gustaffson's house. No signs of damage or of occupancy at any of the locked-up camps. The afternoon rain shower had washed the drive, parking area and steps, but tire tracks showed that a car had recently parked between two of the camps.

Amy heard the unembellished facts delivered unemotionally as Dort paced the long kitchen. She watched his face and the set of his shoulders. ''What else did you learn?''

Dort turned his head to look at her as though surprised to find someone listening to his thoughts. He washed his hands at the kitchen sink before he took the seat opposite Amy, who was ladling out the soup.

''I'm hungry. When I'm thinking, I forget my stomach.'' Dort moved his spoon through the thick soup. ''Cabbage, beans, pork. What is this?''

''*Corba*. A Slovenian bean soup with sauerkraut, potatoes, and pork cubes—the kind of food that fits my lifestyle. I can keep it on simmer when I'm too busy to stop to eat. What happened after you checked the camps?''

''Went to my place for coffee and scrambled eggs and compared notes. When we checked in we found out about name tags or laundry marks the state police had found on the boy's clothing and the identification label inside the pocket of the jacket.''

Amy interrupted. "The jacket belongs to Tim Mozeson, son of my New York publisher, the man I work for."

"How do you know that?"

"I had an appointment to check in with Sam Mozeson at noon," Amy said. "We keep in touch by phone when we're close to deadline. After we finished discussing the book, Sam told me about getting a call from Maine police, about the jacket. Said he and his wife were contacting everyone they know who might have any idea why their son came to Maine and where he might be in the state."

"Was this Tim traveling alone? Is he the same age as the dead body?"

Amy refilled their glasses from the tall, brown-speckled pitcher. Dort ladled more soup into his bowl but held his spoon in the air, waiting for her answer.

"I feel sad. The whole thing's sad. Sam Mozeson has been a business associate for years. My boss but kind of a distant friend. I knew nothing about his private life until today. Sam told me his son is thirty-two, that he stopped in New York on his way to Maine. Where did Tim Mozeson live, Dort? What was the address in the jacket?"

"Cincinnati."

"Ohio to New York to Maine." Amy's fingers tapped her collarbone. "Sam said his son had visited his mother, the son's mother, before coming to Sam's house to see him. He also told me Tim was recently divorced and between jobs."

They ate in silence. Dort spread butter on the heel of the carrot bread, put it in his bowl, and ladled soup over it. Then he carefully cut it into small pieces. Amy smiled as she watched him. "You still do that. When you were twenty-one, my father tried to guess how many loaf ends Dort Adams had soaked in soup.''

"Store bread doesn't count. But a heel of yeast bread is food. Sometimes after dinner, I beat an egg with milk, pour it over the end pieces, and bake them next morning for breakfast. You still bake bread every week?''

"Usually. More to help me think than the need for food. When I knead out my frustrations and anger, really pummel the dough, I end up with fine-grained loaves. My mind works better when my body is busy—gardening, making bread, swimming.''

Amy pointed to the cookie jar on the back side of the table. "Tell me about the marks on the clothing. Did you get information on those last night?''

"Not until this morning,'' Dort said. "Just before I came over and found you hanging. You did that when you were in high school and college. You hung from branches and ladder rungs. Have you been hanging all these years?''

"I told you. Stretching gets the kinks out. Relaxes me. Those laundry marks. What did you find out?''

"One belongs to a college student in Buffalo, New York. The other hasn't been traced yet. The boy may have borrowed clothes. Maybe he had one kind of mark for laundry at home and another at college.'' Dort took small bites from a large oatmeal cookie. "Aren't laundry marks a thing of the past? I think of laundry service for folks with money, summer people or men traveling on business. But college kids…don't they use laundromats? Have wash and wear shirts?''

"That's what I was thinking. The laundries around here went out of business years ago in spite of summer people. Some laundromats have a wash-and-fold service. Do such services use laundry marks?'' Without waiting for a response, Amy asked, "What did the police find from Buffalo and what conclusions are they drawing from that information?"

"The name they have is William R. Stillman, age twenty, sophomore, English major, last seen on campus in Buffalo on Friday afternoon. The stitched-in nametags match one mark used by a western New York laundry and dry cleaning service. College registrar checked his records. No Maine connections in them. Police have not been able to contact his family."

"Family. A mom and dad family?"

"Yes and no. What made you ask that?"

"A feeling. A feeling I've had since I found the body. Nothing logical. Nothing I can explain. It's as though I should know this boy, should recognize him. I know, I know. It doesn't make sense and I'm not trying to have visions. But from my first sight of that boy on the floor of that shed, I've had this feeling that I know something I don't know."

As Amy watched, Dort went "out of town." He frowned as he looked past her, over her shoulder. In this long, old kitchen he was staring at the pantry cupboards. Amy waited. The ringing of the phone brought Dort back, to his feet and alert. Amy held up her hand. "Wait. Let the machine do its job. If that's Polly Anderson with her bigoted gossip, I don't want to listen to which race or religion or politician she's hating today."

But when the sheriff's voice followed the beep, Dort lifted the receiver. He turned to look down at Amy after he hung up. "Bent wants me to take a run up and look around the old Fullerton place. Someone saw lights up there Monday night. Want to ride along?"

They carried their dishes to the sink and rinsed them. Amy covered the Crockpot and set it in the pantry. Dort pushed in the chairs and took another cookie before he moved the blue-and-white jar to the back side of the table. "Is that the same cookie jar your mother used to fill?"

"Same jar. Same cookies. She called them Granton Goobers because she used ground peanuts. I use walnuts or pecans but I soak the raisins overnight like she did." Amy changed her loafers for waterproof boots and put on her flannel-lined denim jacket, the one with five pockets.

By hounds' run, the old Fullerton place was only about a mile away, but because of brooks and swamps, it was a four-mile drive by road. Amy settled back against the well-padded seat and let her mind focus on how different the roadsides appeared from the perspective of the high truck seat, compared with the way she saw them from her low compact.

"Is your ex-husband still alive?"

Amy turned to look at Dort, who was staring straight ahead. "What brought that to mind?"

"Sorry. I just wondered, so I asked."

They rode in silence down through Hurley's Hollow and out toward Moose Brook crossroads. Today, rusty trailers and mobile homes lined the road through Hurley's Hollow. These replaced the shacks and cabins that had housed part of Granton's population in the days when Dort and Amy walked through the countryside, exploring, and arguing about school and life.

"Monty's alive. In Arizona. He and Charlie run an inn that caters to artists. Hank Gustaffson stayed with them when he was out west last winter."

Dort maneuvered the truck around potholes, washouts, and soft shoulders. Amy held onto the edge of the seat and looked down into Sacaja Valley as they neared the top of the hill. Off to the southeast she could see the Morse Mill and the road to the harbor, twisting as it followed the river. Smoke rose from the chimney of a house behind the mill.

"Who lives in that house over east of the mill, where smoke is coming up from that chimney? Is that an East Granton place? Off the East Granton road?"

Dort swung the truck around and parked on an outcropping ledge beside the old farm driveway, below the vacant house. They looked down the peninsula toward Sacaja Harbor with the river and the road visible through the branches of the bare, budded trees.

"That's the Neilson place. Couple from Massachusetts are renting it. Young couple with kids. He's a chef someplace up in Camden. She's been working in the mill office. See the trail behind the mill? East Granton kids use it as an off-road run for their ATVs. Rocky Devons hauls firewood out through there with his tractor." Dort looked at Amy. "Are you thinking what I'm thinking?"

"Another way the boy's body could have been brought to the sawdust shed."

They were silent again as they looked down at the valley and its network of roads. Amy was thinking of those bent and broken willow branches. Snagged in a tractor wheel? But the first question hadn't been answered yet. If the dead boy was William R. Stillman, Buffalo college student, why had he been in Granton, Maine, last Monday?

Dort broke the silence by stepping down from the truck. Amy followed and, standing on the ledge below the old farmhouse, found herself seeing the farm as it had been years ago. Paul Fullerton, the only one of the four brothers who married, had outlived the other three. He had died ten years ago.

"Remember when we first came up here, Dort? That first October? We peeled apples with Lou Fullerton. She was making mincemeat and we sat with her down in the orchard, pitching peelings off into the field while she told us stories about sailing with her father. That was more than thirty years ago. And she lived on this hill with those four brothers for years after that."

"Amy. Over here."

Dort's voice came from the other side of the fenced-in farmhouse yard where he stood before the open barn door. A mound of dark fur lay on the ground before him.

FIVE

"GET SOME WATER. Somewhere. Quickly." Dort shouted out orders while he struggled to remove the dog's collar. The large, long-haired dog lay at the end of a chain that stretched deep inside the barn. A slight movement, a weak lift of the dog's tail told her the animal was still alive.

Lou's garden pool. The pool Louella Fullerton had chiseled and chipped out, enlarging a depression in the ledge. Drifted leaves had almost obscured it but there was water. Using the tin collapsible cup from an inside jacket pocket, Amy brought water to drip onto the dog's tongue.

"See if there's a pan inside." Dort took the cup. With his right hand he let drops of water fall into the dog's mouth. He slid his left hand gently under the animal's head and raised it up from the ground to let the dripping fluid run back toward its throat. Once again the dirt-encrusted tail moved, a slight flutter.

There were no pans or dishes to be seen inside the dark, cobwebbed barn. Amy followed the chain to the post on which it was fastened. No sign that the dog had been given food or water at any time after it had been chained there. She refilled the cup from the pool in the ledge and watched Dort continue to drip the water slowly onto the dog's tongue. The tail fluttered again.

They waited in silence until the dog's throat moved. Dort shifted his position so the dog's head was between his knees, murmuring softly as he lifted the animal's head a bit more to let the drops roll to the back of the tongue. Another throat movement. More slow drops.

"Do you think he's injured?" Amy asked. "Hurt beyond no food and water?"

"I don't know. I don't see any blood. His legs aren't bent. We need to get him down to Doc Kelling. There's a tarp in the back of the pickup. We can slip that under him and slide him into the truck. I'll back up to the barn ramp." Dort rubbed the dog's head and ears and continued to let water trickle very slowly into its mouth until the cup was empty.

Amy insisted on riding in the bed of the pickup with the dog to keep him from shifting or sliding as they went back down the rough hill road. She scratched the top of his head and talked to him. Dog talk. Reassuring tones. She looked back up the hill. They hadn't checked the house. Hadn't looked beyond the doorway of the barn.

Who would leave a dog chained without attention? How long had the animal been without food and water, straining to get loose? Had an accident kept the owner from returning? But there had been no evidence that even a bowl of water had been left for the dog. This was disturbing. As immediately disturbing as her finding the body of a college student from a campus in western New York in Morse's sawdust shed. Two odd incidents. Both stirred Amy to question, "Why?" Had William Stillman come to Granton to meet someone? Had someone deliberately left this dog to suffer, chained in the barn of an unoccupied farmhouse?

Amy hardly noticed the landscape. Her hands continued to stroke the dog's head while her mind skittered

from wondering who owned the Fullerton place now—
there were no FOR SALE signs—to where in Maine Tim
Mozeson might be and what kind of tool had smashed
the skull of a twenty-year-old stranger. Could it have
been an accident? A hiker's fall?

Doc Kelling and Ruth Waldron came out as Dort
pulled into the veterinary hospital drive. That car phone
again. Doc listened to the dog's heart and breathing, ran
his fingers along the spine and over each leg. Ruth held
a stretcher, upright, by her side.

"Let's get her inside."

"Her?" Dort and Amy said it almost in unison.

"I treated this dog last week," Doc Kelling said.
"She's three years old. Part collie, part black lab,
spayed, nice dog. We'll give her fluid intravenously and,
if there are no other injuries, she'll recover. But I want
to know who's responsible for this, who abused this
dog."

"Who owns him…her?" Amy asked.

Dort reached for the stretcher. Amy and Ruth pulled
the tarp. The two men shifted the big dog onto the
stretcher and lifted it. Ruth held the door open.

Amy was waiting in the truck when Dort came out
and, in answer to his, "Hill or home?" she pointed toward the hill. For the third time within an hour, Dort
drove through Hurley's Hollow, past dead cars and rust-
ing trailers squatting in rubbish-strewn yards. When they
turned at Moose Crossing to head up to the Fullerton
farm again, Dort took a deep breath and began to talk.
In response to his call to the sheriff's office, made on
the drive to the vet's, Bent was coming to Granton. Dort
was to check through the barn and behind it as well as
around the house.

"Who owns the dog?"

"New man at the harbor. Maybe one of your Old Baptists. Doc has his name in the records. I didn't wait. Man moved here in March, lives alone, takes good care of the animal. Doc can't figure any possible reason why that dog would be in the Fullerton barn. How would a newcomer even know about the place?"

"Those lights people saw Monday night," Amy said, "were they moving lights, glowing lights, or what Hank Gustaffson said he saw—lights in windows where you didn't expect to see lights?"

"Bent says the office received three calls. A woman reported seeing lights inside the farmhouse. The other two callers asked what was going on up on Fullerton Hill. They described what they saw as searchlights or headlight beams, aimed at the barn. Those callers said they were concerned about vandalism and fire."

"Wait a minute." Amy turned so she could watch Dort's face. "Did these three calls come in on Monday night? Or were they after the news of finding the body was broadcast on Wednesday, after folks were asked to supply information, to report anything that may have struck them as being unusual?"

"One call Monday night. Sheriff's patrol on Route One drove down Granton Road until they could see the hilltop and called in to say all was dark, no sign of lights. They didn't drive up. They'd been checking on damage to boats being hauled from winter storage. The other two calls came in Wednesday after the news broadcast request."

He parked the truck on the ledge below the ramp to the front of the barn. Dort and Amy paused to sniff and listen before moving in through the open barn door. Dort's flashlight showed the chain looped around the first center post. If the dog had had food and water, she could have been comfortable in the barn with space to move about and piles of hay for warm sleeping.

By the time Bent Woodman and his deputy drove in, Dort had checked the hayloft and Amy had walked through the milking parlor and the grain room and checked the back chutes built to carry manure down to the storage pits. They found signs of temporary visitations of couples seeking privacy, probably last summer, but layers of undisturbed dust and cobwebs in all doorways indicated that no one had been roaming through the barn recently.

Sheriff Woodman brought a search warrant and a key to the house, obtained from the lawyer who paid the taxes last year. Before going in, the four of them walked around the old farmhouse, a high-posted Cape Cod structure with a large, square ell added at the center back. Amy noticed that the shades in seven of the windows of the main part of the house were pulled down to six inches below the overlap of the bottom and top sashes. In the eighth window, facing east, the shade was raised as were those on the six windows of the kitchen ell. The single window of the attic above the kitchen had no shade. Dort noticed fresh woodchuck holes below the front steps.

The key opened the door into the kitchen, a square room with windows on three sides, views of the rolling hills off to the west, of barn and pastures on the north and, to the east, of the road winding out through East Granton. Young pines, taking over the neglected hayfields, cut off most of the view of Ward's Pond. The Fullerton farm was isolated but the world spread out on every side.

A center hall divided the main house. Steep stairs, parallel to the hall, rose just four feet back from the

wide, double front door that faced south. The rooms followed the traditional Cape Cod floor plan—two large
rooms in front and two smaller rooms behind them, next
to the kitchen. The window shade in the small room on
the east was rolled up a foot above the center sash as
though a tall person stood there to look out.

At the doorway to this room, Amy held out her arm
to halt the men. "There's mud on the carpet under that
window. Mud in front of that Morris chair. Something
smells odd or fresh. Different, not like the air in the
kitchen."

Across the hall the cellar door was ajar. Narrow, steep
stairs went down directly under the staircase to the second floor. Fresh air from an open cellar window? Dort
and the sheriff went down.

Amy moved toward the front door. Both front rooms
had been used as bedrooms. Had that small, cramped,
one-window room been the sitting room for Louella and
the four Fullerton men? Or had they spent their leisure
hours in the kitchen? Had Lou Fullerton had any space
of her own?

The sidelights of the front door allowed sunlight from
the south into this hall through winters and summers.
The striped strip of carpeting on the stairs was faded and
worn. Amy held one arm before her face to push away
cobwebs as she moved up to the second floor. Two more
bedrooms. Rooms with low ceilings but each with two
windows. Windows with old, brittle green shades, neatly
pulled down to six inches below the center. And one
more room, over the kitchen ell—a small, dark room,
narrowed by the sloping roof. The one window, facing
north toward the barn, had neither shade nor curtains.

Old trunks and boxes filled the end of the room by
the door from the upstairs hallway. Boxes stacked on

boxes, higher than Amy's head, touched the beams of the sloping roof. The approach toward the window was like moving forward through a tunnel. Amy moved toward it, stepping quietly on the worn straw matting. Moved through to the open end of the room where a brightly colored braided rug lay on the dull, neutral floor covering. Where a tall easel, with a soft blue cloth draped over it, stood centered upon that bright rug in that attic space. Whose space?

Canvases, dozens and dozens of canvases, leaned against each other along the side of the room, turned so only their blank backs could be seen. Amy moved forward, hesitated, and then lifted the blue drape away from the canvas on the easel.

SIX

THE WARMTH OF COLOR in the painting and the feelings of joy emanating from the figures caught Amy's whole being. Tears filled her eyes, her breath caught in her throat. A man and woman, apart but intimate, facing each other with their hands on each other's shoulders, bathed in the undulating glow of sunlit, red-gold maple leaves. Amy's mind and body remembered that lift of vibrant closeness once felt in the glory of an October day.

Her hand let the blue drape fall to cover the painting. Tears slid down her cheeks as she stood motionless, eyes closed, breathing deeply. Her habit of asking questions, of herself and others, was arrested, drowned in feelings and memories. Amy Creighton stood alone in the attic of the long-empty Fullerton farmhouse, looking back down the years to wild and wonderful autumn days when she was Amy Wainwright, young and alive, when she had known and shared the warmth and intimacy so vividly portrayed in that painting.

"Are you OK?"

How could a 220-pound man move so quietly? Amy looked up at Dort, her eyes still swimming in tears. She didn't answer. Sheriff Woodman, having come from between the trunks and boxes, watched his constable and Amy and waited for one of them to speak.

Dort reached out and let his hand rest on Amy's shoulder, lightly, the same gentle touch he had used to steady and comfort that suffering dog. When he spoke his voice was low and quiet. "Someone has been coming into the house. Through the root cellar, through the outside entrance, and then into the house cellar. Recently. The dirt on the carpet looks like that from the bulkhead steps. The state police lab crew is on its way."

Amy dug tissues from one of the jacket pockets and wiped away her tears. Bentley Woodman looked from Dort to Amy.

"Who painted all this?" Bent gestured toward the stacked canvases. He picked up the one nearest to him and turned it so the light from the window made it possible for all three to see. Wind-drifted leaves lay in ragged, sodden piles against a rough stone wall that sloped down behind the naked boles of winter trees. No snow but a feeling of cold and silence.

"One of the Fullertons paint this?" Bent directed his question to both Amy and Dort.

"That's the pasture wall below the house, east of the house. We hunted pheasants in that field." Dort turned to Amy. "You climbed those trees, hung on those branches."

Amy lifted the blue cloth again from the painting on the easel and heard Dort gasp softly. Bent moved around behind her for a full view. "That's the same spot in a different season. Same wall. Same low branch in the foreground." He held up the winter scene still in his hands. "Were these painted recently?"

"Not this month, if that's what you're asking. But not twenty or thirty years ago." Dort stepped back but continued to look at the easel painting. "When did Paul Fullerton die? How long ago?"

"Ten years ago," Amy said. "In the summer. The year they built the new bridge at Moose Crossing. There was one-way traffic the day folks drove up here for the funeral meats."

"How long has the house been vacant?" Bent looked from Dort to Amy. Their eyes were focused on that warm, joyful October scene.

"They sold the stock before Paul died," Amy said. "That first winter Louella stayed here alone. A cousin or friend came to stay with her the next summer. I can't tell you when she left. I don't hear much village news. I dropped out of social doings. So did Lou Fullerton. I don't know who her friends were. I do know she had no relatives in Maine."

"Did she paint? Are these hers?" Bent turned two more canvases around—two paintings of a tall, stooped figure moving off through mist into the woods, pines among leafless trees, a puddle-spotted trail winding past a lichen-covered boulder. "These have a gloomy, melancholy tone. Were the Fullertons unhappy people?"

Dort and Amy both shook their heads. "The Fullerton men were silent types. They seldom smiled," Dort said. "But I never thought of them as unhappy. When we knew Lou, when we used to come up here, she was a cheerful, happy woman. Alert, full of ideas and observations. Alive. But that was more than thirty years ago. She lived up here with those four brothers, no close neighbors and—I don't know. Maybe she did change. Maybe she did become miserable."

Amy added, "Lou walked a lot, down through those trails among the trees. One year she showed me her path to Ward's Pond and we cut a shortcut around the swamp to my parent's land, now my place. After that I used that path to come up here." Amy turned to the stacked canvases and began tipping them forward, taking quick looks. She lifted one for the two men to see. "This is along that trail. Lou Fullerton planted those white birches there below the pines. The pines were young trees then, seeding in along the hillside."

"Why did you stop coming up here, stop being neighborly? Did something happen?" Bent Woodman asked.

"We went off to college and then we went away to work," Dort told him. "We didn't see how we could earn a living here in Granton. I went to Arizona. Amy went to work in New York."

The lab van could be heard rattling over the ledges by the barn. As they turned and started out through the tunnel of stored boxes, the sheriff spoke over his shoulder. "You still haven't told me who painted. Who is still painting."

Woodman's deputy called from the lower hallway to say the lab crew driver was at the kitchen door. Bent Woodman went down. But he paused with his hand on the newel post and frowned at Dort and Amy. "You know more than you're telling me. I'll talk with both of you later."

SEVEN

AMY MOVED ASIDE at the foot of the back steps to let the police lab crew carry up their equipment. The old path across the east field was clearly visible, a green line through the tawny, winter-killed grass of the pasture. At the bottom of the slope, two old maple trees stood before the stone wall, the same wall, the same trees they had looked at in the sad and somber paintings and in that vibrant October scene.

She was reaching up, rubbing her hands along the lowest branch, before she realized she had crossed the field. There, just behind the largest tree, were the remains of the stile Louella had built, or one like it, double steps to get up and over the wide stone wall. And beyond that wall, the path to Ward's Pond. The nursery rhyme words brought a smile. "Pig won't go over the stile and I shan't get home tonight." Lou Fullerton had named her dog Porcine because he howled every time Lou went over the stile.

The black flies brought Amy back to the present. Up by the house, hilltop breezes hindered their flight but, down here under the great maples, the small nasty flies crawled on and bit all exposed skin surfaces. Amy wiped the clustering creatures away from her face and started back up the slope. Flashes of past years came and went. Coming up through this field in July with Lou waving

from among the flamboyant colors of her flower beds.
Joyful memories of young Amy Wainwright walking,
running, flying up this path, up to that house on golden
October afternoons. A desolate memory of moving
slowly up this slope on that gray November day when
she came to say goodbye before leaving Granton.

Ahead of her, on the east side of the main house, was
that one window with the raised shade. Amy turned. Yes,
the leafless trees and the mist beyond the stone wall had
been painted from this side of the house. Seen or remembered.

Dort and the sheriff came out of the barn and Amy
walked across the farmyard to meet them. Cobwebs
stretched along the shoulders of Bent's brown uniform
and one, caught on Dort's cap, fluttered in the breeze.
The men stopped beside the dog's collar on the end of
the chain.

"Why was a dog from the harbor chained up in this
barn?" Dort asked. "And if three people saw lights up
here on Monday night, what kind of creep wouldn't give
a dog some water? They should have let him go."

Dort didn't wait for an answer. He turned to Amy.
"Let's go. We'll see what Doc Kelling can tell us before
I question your Old Baptist."

"Old Baptist?" Bent asked.

"It's a long story. All it adds up to is that a new
reporter mixed up his facts in writing a Sacaja story.
Mixed his information about newcomers at the harbor
and the Coffin Cove church they want to restore. As a
result, that group is now called the Old Baptists. Doc
Kelling says one of them owned the dog we found."

Sheriff Woodman waved both hands in a "what's
next" gesture and went to join his men on the farmhouse
steps. Amy and Dort started back to town. After the

potholes and bumps of the hill had been negotiated, Dort said, "You walked down to the wall."

"Yes." Amy made no other response.

Hurley's Hollow had come to life. Children and dogs raced across grass and driveways and around the pickup trucks and cars now parked beside the trailers. Dort braked to avoid two boys chasing a soccer ball, waved in response to their shouts and then slowed again. "What's Joe Waldron doing out here?"

"Where? I don't see him." Amy could see no adults on either side of the road.

"His truck," said Dort, pointing to a new, heavy-duty pickup with oversized tires. "That's Mel Driscoll's trailer but Mel's truck's not there."

"Maybe his truck's in for repairs again and Joe brought him home. I gave Mel a ride back to town last week when his truck died coming down Route One."

"His truck was running this morning."

Dort turned right onto the cut-through to Granton Road and then made another right turn down a long driveway toward the river. He grinned at Amy. "Comfort stop."

Amy had passed Dort's house many times while canoeing on the river but had never viewed it from the land side. The Sacaja River looped around a high section of the shore as it flowed through the intervales. Dort's house sat on that high ground, looking up and down the river.

East and west of this higher point, the fields were farmed. A surveyor's error a hundred years ago had resulted in a dispute over a narrow strip of land from the main road to the river. While the property owners on both sides argued and went to court, trees grew on the land between the two farms. By the time that parcel of land had a clear title, the holder of that title was dead and his heirs were in court for a probate review.

According to local gossip, Dort Adams happened to be in the county courthouse the day Phil Buckley's relatives from Michigan were there, trying to tie up all the loose ends of his estate, including the farm in Granton. Dort helped them speed up the settlement. He bought the tree-covered strip and built his house on the point before town ordinances set wider requirements for house lots. That was after his wife left him. And it was after Montgomery Creighton left her. Fifteen years ago?

Dort's old dog, too old and lame to climb in and out of the truck any longer, bent himself almost in half wriggling in welcome. He whined with pleasure when Dort scooched down to rub his ears. Amy scratched the old lab under his chin as she surveyed the yard and river. The shingled house, long and low, stretched along the dairy farm's pasture fence.

"Come in." Dort held the door. "I need a cup of coffee. Bathroom's on the left. Second door."

They carried their coffee to the table in front of the windows overlooking the river. Dort set a bowl of crackers, a plate of cheese, and two knives between them.

"Let's go back to where we were at lunch," he said. He looked at his watch. "Whoops. I'd better call Doc Kelling first. It's after six o'clock."

When he came back to the table he told Amy the dog was doing well. "The Old Baptist who owns her, Alex Beaufort, is driving up at seven. Says he never heard of the Fullerton farm. Told Doc he had advertised for his missing dog. How does that sound to you?"

"Beaufort? Wasn't there a Beaufort family lived on Bean Island? No, that was Beaulard. My father talked about bootlegging days and the Bean Island families.

Tales of men found drowned out there with bashed heads but somehow no charges were ever made."

Amy tapped her fingers against her collarbone. "How does the dog story sound to me? It's easy enough to check the paper, find out when that ad was phoned in. But I'm thinking of someone really wicked and evil, someone so unfeeling they would chain a dog in an isolated place and go off, leaving the creature without water and food. I'm thinking of the lights on Monday night— up at the farm and over on Sacaja Pond. But mostly I'm centered on how that boy died. I keep seeing his face." She shook her head. "Have you and the sheriff considered a connection between the chained dog and William Stillman's death? Are the police sure that boy was Stillman?"

"The college records, fingerprints, and photos came through. He is Stillman. About the lights—the sheriff's department and the state police both want to know what was going on Monday night," Dort said. "And on Sunday night. Who was out on local roads, what they saw. Eb Simmons checked cars and drivers bringing kids back from the music program. Two boys thought they saw a truck parked by Morse Mill, in the drive by the office. A girl in the same car thinks there was a car in the driveway of Ira Bellhouse's place. Olive Anderson was driving. She slowed down near the mill because they almost hit a skunk there on their way down."

"Who's checking hotels and motels? Wouldn't someone from Buffalo be registered somewhere?"

"Not if he came with someone or to meet someone."

Amy considered this. "But you said there was no Maine connection in William Stillman's college records. What about his family? Did you locate them?"

Dort refilled their coffee mugs and stood holding and

patting the thermos which had produced good coffee so quickly. "Amy Creighton, other places have messed-up, mixed-up families just as Granton does." He touched Amy's shoulder and pointed to the opposite shore of the river where a doe and her fawn were slipping down to the sand strip to drink. "Bent told me they located Stillman's father at a hunting lodge in South Carolina. With his secretary. The boy's mother and a friend, a male friend, were in Philadelphia. Neither parent had seen their son since Christmas.

"According to college records, Stillman seldom left the campus. During spring break, he worked shifts in the library so a classmate could go home for the week." Dort paused. "That sounds very nice, but something doesn't ring true. From information the campus security office and Buffalo police have put together, Stillman was seen at the college at noon on Friday. He was dead in Granton, Maine, Monday night. His body wasn't found until Wednesday morning and yet no one seems to have noticed that he wasn't around, wasn't on campus, at meals, or in classes during those five days. No one reported him missing."

"Dates? Girlfriends?"

"No. No boyfriends, either. No athletic activities. No music group participation. Stillman seems to have been a loner."

"Then what did he do? He was there on campus for almost two years. Someone must have noticed how a good looking, healthy college sophomore spent his time. Egad...at that age I used to walk twelve or fifteen miles, eat like a pig, and walk back. Not just because I grew up hiking over Maine hills. Lots of us walked that way. It was a high energy period, being twenty and being alive. Someone must have known this boy. Was he called Bill or was he a William?''

''Does it matter?''

''It would tell something about him. Remember Margaret Tatetrau?''

''Yes. But what's your point?''

''Margaret's mother wouldn't allow anyone to call her daughter by a nickname or a silly name, even in games at birthday parties. Margaret was to be Margaret. The first time she ran away from home, they found her in South Carolina. 'Maggie' Tatetrau was working as a waitress. The next time, she was found in Chicago using the name Peggy. She's now Meg Aronson, doing public relations for a museum in Virginia. Definitely not a Margaret.''

Dort put the thermos back in the kitchen. As he rewrapped the cheese, he asked, ''You think Sonny Prim might be less of a wimp if his grandmother hadn't stuck him with that Sonny? Was he ever called Walter or Walt by anyone?''

''Sonny Prim and Junie Carson. Little Junior,'' Amy said. ''I don't think I ever heard either one of them called by their names. I have an ingrained revulsion about the names some parents stick on little kids. Just as I feel uncomfortable when I see or think I see domineering characters controlling weaker, trapped individuals, not letting them grow. I expect explosions. Sudden reactions or rebellions. And usually, the wrong people get hurt.''

She carried her mug and the bowl of crackers back to the kitchen. ''That's my soap box speech for the day. But I'd feel better if that boy was Bill. I'd feel better if I knew someone missed him.''

As they headed out the long driveway, Dort looked

down at Amy and asked, "Want to know what Old Baptist Beaufort named that dog?"

"Please."

"Margaret!"

EIGHT

"MARGARET! No one names a dog Margaret. That's worse than Rover or Spot. Where did Beaufort get the dog? Did he bring her with him? You said he came here in March."

Amy was almost sputtering and Dort was enjoying the response he had triggered. "Why do names bend you out of shape?" he asked. "First you want the murder victim to be called Bill and now you're in a tizzy because the Old Baptist named his dog Margaret. Next you'll tell me the Sacaja River should be called the Little Thames or something."

"Dort Adams, I don't have tizzies. Snits, maybe, but tizzies, no. Would you name a dog Margaret?"

"No. I associate the name Margaret with straight-backed librarians, maiden aunts, and women who starch pillow cases," Dort said. "Priscillas wear ruffles and shriek at the sight of mice and anyone named Dorothy can be trusted with money. You're not the only one with illogical feelings about names. I wanted to see if I could ruffle your cold calm."

Before Amy could respond, they pulled up in front of Doc Kelling's. Dort stepped out before Amy had a chance to voice her opinion. She did not like being called cold.

Joe Waldron's big truck was parked in the street,

blocking the driveway. In the waiting room, Waldron stood before the desk, rocking on his heels. A stranger—an older, dark-haired man—sat across the room, watching. "That's quite a truck, Joe," Dort said. "What're you planning to haul?"

"Nothing special," Joe answered. "I just don't like lightweight trucks. This'll be good on hills in the winter."

"What kind of mileage?"

"About fifteen miles per gallon. But I don't go far."

"Your kids too young to drive? Still in school here or up at the high school?" Dort sat down beside Amy but Joe remained standing. He looked annoyed, either at waiting or at Dort's questions.

"One boy here in Granton. Older boy up at the high school. They won't be driving for a few more years and then they won't drive this truck. No one drives it but me." Doc Kelling came in from the treating room, nodded at Joe, at Dort and Amy, and turned to the stranger. "Margaret's going to be fine, Mr. Beaufort, but she'll need to stay here overnight. She was seriously dehydrated and she's going to need a bath."

"You're sure she's going to be OK? I don't think I know how to take care of a sick dog."

Dort interrupted. "Mr. Beaufort, I'm Dort Adams, Granton constable. The sheriff would like me to ask you some questions about your dog. Can we do this now?"

Before Beaufort could answer, Ruth Waldron came out into the waiting room and her husband said, "Come on. I'm waiting. Let's go. I want my supper."

"Joe, this is Thursday. I don't get through until eight."

Doc Kelling said, "We're running a bit late today,

Joe. And the state police are coming back for more information.''

Joe ignored the veterinarian and spoke directly to Ruth. ''I think you better find a job with better hours.'' And without a word or nod to anyone else, he walked out.

Beaufort watched Joe Waldron go out and then turned back to Doc Kelling. ''My dog has better manners.''

When Ruth told Beaufort he could come in and see his dog, Dort and Amy asked if they could join him.

The dog was strapped to a treating table so the intravenous fluids could continue to drip into her veins, but she lifted her head and flapped her tail. The inert mass of dirty fir had become a responsive animal. Dort and Amy stroked and scratched and talked to her. Beaufort stood back, shuddering at the sight of the fluid bottle, tube, and needle.

Dort moved back first. ''Sorry, sir. We've been monopolizing your dog. Come on over.''

''Thanks. I'm not good with illnesses, with sick people or animals. I'll see her tomorrow.''

''But she needs love and attention now,'' Amy said.

''I don't do that well,'' Beaufort said. He moved toward the door. ''You had some questions, Mr. Adams?''

Dort and Alex Beaufort returned to the waiting room. Ruth checked the fluid gauge and then went on to care for the other animals recovering in cages in the back room. Amy turned to Doc Kelling but continued to stroke Margaret.

''How long do you think this dog was without water?'' she asked. ''Up there without water and food? When did Beaufort say he first missed the dog?''

Doc Kelling patted Margaret's hindquarters gently and said, ''Beaufort told me he first missed the dog on Saturday. Margaret didn't appear for food or for their evening stroll. He's not really a dog person. Thought he needed a watch dog when he moved down there on the peninsula so he chose this one from what they had that week at the Humane Society's place in Camden. That was in March. Brought her in for shots. Brought her in again about three weeks ago when she cut her foot on broken glass along the road. The man seemed more upset about blood stains in his car than he did about Margaret's stitches.''

Kelling ran his index finger down the dog's nose. Margaret considered this a splendid sign of affection and gave out a soft, whirring whine. ''See how her throat is recovering? This dog craves attention,'' he said. ''Maybe a nice fifty-year-old blond who likes to cook would be more suitable company for Alex Beaufort at his seaside place.''

''How long, how many days, do you think this dog was chained up with no water?'' Amy asked again.

''Four or five,'' answered Kelling. ''Depends on how much struggling or straining she did. Wicked way to treat an animal. Any idea who goes up to the Fullerton place? Or why?''

''Not yet. That's one thing the sheriff is trying to find out,'' said Amy. ''You took care of the Fullerton farm animals, didn't you? Has Lou Fullerton been coming back here summers? She wouldn't stay up there without a dog.''

''No. She wouldn't. But Lou and Graham Ford stay at his place most of the time. They didn't have a dog last summer. Brought a cat in one day to be put to sleep, a stray they found in the barn, hurt and sick. You remember how Lou felt about hurt animals. The first patient I had in Granton when I opened this office was a lamb she brought in. Not hers. She was driving by Mart Morse's pasture, noticed the lamb caught on his barbed wire fence, snagged it up and brought it to me. Wonderful woman.''

"Graham Ford? The artist with the summer place over on Ward's Pond?''

"Yes. He taught Lou to paint and encouraged her— before or after Paul died. She's doing well. Paintings in exhibits out west where they lived in winter. Last year they stayed at the pond until the middle of October. She told me nothing anywhere matches October colors in Sacaja Valley but she never wants to see a gaunt November in Maine again. Living with those four dour Fullerton brothers couldn't have been a very joyful existence.''

Amy's hands continued to stroke Margaret's ears while she tried to fit these unexpected bits of information into a mind that had stopped thinking of the Fullertons years ago. "But Lou must be seventy years old.''

"You're suggesting that living and loving stop at some mathematical point?" Doc Kelling was laughing at her confusion.

But he didn't know the depth of her confusion. From the moment Amy lifted the blue drape on that easel, whole segments of the life she thought she'd put behind her, put securely away, had been slipping back. Everything that had happened since she and Dort drove up to the Fullerton farm had stirred recollections, stirred confusing emotions. Did she believe that feelings congealed at some arbitrary, abstract age? That there was an age or time when there was no longer any hope of experiencing again that wild, warm aliveness? Her reactions to that October painting...

"I won't ask why you and Dort Adams live in single,

solitary states. Granton folks still talk about the two of you, together winter and summer through all your school and college years. I'm as curious as the rest of the town. What happened? Did it take a murder to get you two to talk to each other again?''

Before Amy could gather her scattered thoughts and respond, Dort called from the doorway, "Doc, the state police are here. Can you and Ruth stop what you're doing and come out?''

NINE

DORT AND AMY listened as the state police questioned Doc Kelling and Ruth Waldron. How long did they think the dog had been chained in the barn? It couldn't have been more than six days if Beaufort had walked with the dog Friday night in Sacaja Harbor.

The veterinarian had found traces of clay on the dog's skin. This indicated that, sometime before the dog was chained up, it had been wet and had lain or rolled in some clay material. This could have been while being transported to the Fullerton farm, perhaps in a vehicle that had previously hauled clay soil, bags of cement, or old bricks. No vegetation that might provide information had been found in the matted fur or on the dog's feet. Neither Doc Kelling nor his assistant had any explanations for why a dog, missing from the harbor, was found chained in a barn on a hill near Route One.

Dort turned his pickup around and headed toward Amy's house. Neither of them spoke until the truck crossed the bridge over Ward's Pond outlet. ''Did you know Lou Fullerton and Graham Ford have been living together? At his place on Ward's Pond in summer and out west in the winter?'' Amy asked.

''Yes.''

''Why didn't you say something when we were at the farm? Have you told Bent Woodman?'' Amy turned to look at Dort but couldn't read his expression. When had Dort Adams developed that blank mask? Was it to protect his thoughts?

"Bent knows Lou and Graham," Dort said. "He hadn't connected the Louella Fullerton he and his wife meet at art show receptions and gallery openings with the Lou Fullerton we talked about, the woman who lived all those years up on that hill farm, cooking and waiting on the four Fullerton men. That was before Bent's time, before he became sheriff."

Dort glanced at Amy. "Bent and his wife own one of Lou's paintings—a western one of canyons. Those gloomy paintings and the Fullerton name set him on the right track but he can't believe the Louella Fullerton he knows painted what we saw this afternoon. He wants to know if the canvases in that attic room were painted before or after Paul Fullerton died. He's trying not to go astray, not to get off track on the murder investigation. Bent's probably wondering as you are, now, about Lou's walks down to Ward's Pond, years ago, when she showed you that path."

Chutney raced and yelped and whirled around the truck until Amy held up her hand and commanded, "Stay!" She calmed the dog with firm strokes and a few "good dog" phrases before she walked around to unlock the door.

"You always use the front door?" Dort asked.

"It's the one nearest my garage," Amy said. "You remember the old road circled back to the barn and then everyone used the door into the kitchen. I had the barn torn down rather than continue to pay for repairs and insurance every year. The Leonards hauled off the beams and good timbers I didn't need and built that house up on Beechman Hill. When the Olson brothers built my

garage and garden workroom, I had it located up front.
Less plowing and shoveling in the winter. So now I use
the front door.''

Chutney dashed inside on a search-and-make-safe
mission. Dort followed Amy, who turned on lights as
she moved through to the kitchen. The light on the answering machine was blinking. A beeping signal
sounded from Amy's office.

"Can you eat soup again?"

"Why not?"

"Heat it in the microwave, in the orange bowls."
Amy brought the Crockpot out of the pantry and pointed
to the bowls they had left by the sink. "That beeping is
probably Sam Mozeson. He said he'd call this evening."
She headed for her office, shrugging out of her jacket as
she went.

Sam's voice on the recording asked her to call him at
his home number. She dialed the number he gave her
and before Sam answered, Dort came down the hall and
stood in the doorway. Amy gestured toward the green
wing chair opposite her desk and switched on the phone
amplifier.

She identified herself and Sam began speaking.
"Amy, my son is on his way to your house. I talked
with him about an hour ago. When he called from Bath,
after he heard the news on his car radio, I suggested he
talk with you and find out, if he could, what's going on
before he checked in with the Maine state police. I
couldn't get an answer from your business number or
your home phone."

"We just came in, Sam. We also want to find out
what the sheriff and the police have learned today. Hear
the results of the autopsy."

"We? Who's with you? I expected to find you at

home. Why were you out so long?" This was not the professional, in-control, reserved Sam Mozeson Amy had known for eight years.

Dort's eyebrows went up and he grinned at her, waiting to witness Amy Creighton's response to that demanding voice. She answered quietly. "The Granton constable is here with me, Sam. One thing led to another all afternoon, some as a result of the murder investigation. We've just come in. We haven't eaten. We're tired and hungry. Did you find out how Bill Stillman, the murdered boy, happened to be wearing your son's jacket?"

"Bill, is it?" whispered Dort.

Sam said, "Tim will tell you the whole story. He met the young man at a restaurant stop on the Maine Turnpike and offered him a lift to Wiscasset. It was raining and getting cooler so he told the kid to put on that jacket. Told him his name, Tim's name, was written inside so the boy could mail it back. Later, he remembered that it was his Ohio address printed in the jacket pocket."

"What other address did he have?" Amy's editing habit picked up on specifics. Tim Mozeson, according to his father, was in the process of moving. Before Sam could respond, Amy said, "Your son was leaving Bath about an hour ago to come here. Was he going to make any stops on the way?"

Amy looked across her desk at Dort, who was rubbing his stomach and making spoon-to-mouth gestures. Maybe it was hunger and fatigue, maybe the tensions of their afternoon experiences, but at that moment Amy felt as though she and Dort were in league against a stranger on the phone. She imitated Dort's spooning gestures.

"When I talked with Tim at eight p.m., he said he would start for Granton right away." Sam paused and then said, "Amy, I'm sorry I was rude. It's none of my business where you were or why." Another longer pause. "I'm not myself. I haven't been since that first call from the Maine state police when I thought Tim had been killed. I've been sitting here feeling powerless. Nothing I have—money, the business—are important compared with my son's safety. But I feel useless. If I disappeared, if I were missing for a month, the only people who'd notice would be those waiting for paychecks."

"I know that feeling—being unknown, invisible." Amy watched Dort's face. Only a slight nod indicated a response to her words. Amy's answer to Sam was spoken to Dort Adams. "That's how I felt when my marriage ended. How I felt for months. But Sam, you know now that your son is alive. Everything is fine."

"No, it isn't. My son is a stranger. Thinking that he was dead—even for a moment—jolted me into seeing that. Tim's problems are my fault, a result of my neglect. I'm fifty-seven years old and I've failed at living."

"Don't be so hard on yourself, Sam. You know you're a damned good publisher. That's not much balm tonight when you're feeling helpless, not able to do anything specific. But Sam, you do know you're important to many, to me. We depend on your wisdom and expertise. Can I reach you at this number, later, after Dort and I have talked to your son?"

"Where else would I be? Yes, Amy, I'll be here. Please do call me." Sam hung up.

Dort headed for the kitchen. "I'll zap the soup again. Where's the bread?"

By the time Amy had given Chutney her supper on the back steps, Dort had the steaming orange bowls on the table. They ate in silence. Amy spoke first. "Do we know any more than we did at lunch time? Does what we know make any sense?'' She watched Dort's face, once again a blank mask, and then added, ''You know more than I do. That Fullerton-Ford relationship. Have I really been keeping myself that isolated?''

''You and I pick up different signals,'' Dort said. ''We always did. Most of our arguments started because we saw and heard the same things differently. Yesterday and today we've been picking up pieces of three different puzzles. The abused dog. The lights seen Monday night. And the murder.''

''And I'm feeling the three are related. I know. I know. It doesn't make sense. Call it a hunch. Call it intuition. Maybe it's brain rot. But I work with words, trying to make sense out of clumps of confusion. This makes me want to find one pattern under all these weird, cluttery happenings. Things not expected in Granton, on this peninsula. My head expects me to discover missing pieces so I can make connections. So I can see what I feel I know.''

Dort put his spoon down and leaned back. ''Let's start with my seeing three puzzles and your feeling they're related, one weird happening. Let's talk and not argue. And listen. Maybe this Tim Mozeson will tell us why Stillman was on his way from Buffalo, New York, to Granton, Maine. Do we know he was headed for Granton? But let's start with how that dog got from Beaufort's place near the harbor to the Fullerton barn.''

''She's a friendly dog. She wasn't tied or fenced,'' Amy said. ''Alex Beaufort is a cold fish. The dog probably responded to anyone who took time to talk to her. Wait. Doc Kelling said Beaufort had only had the dog since March. Maybe before that she rode around in pickup trucks, hopped in the way your dog used to. We don't know how far she roamed from Beaufort's place. I doubt if he knows."

Dort carried Amy's thoughts a step further. "Kelling told the state police he believed the dog had been wet before lying on or rolling in some kind of clay material. If we consider a pickup that had carried bags of cement or clay soil and a dog wandering in the rain... What was the weather last Friday night? When did we get those soaking showers?"

Chutney's barking interrupted them. Amy went to answer the knocking on the front door.

TEN

"MRS. CREIGHTON? I'm Tim Mozeson."

Chutney stopped barking but blocked the doorway until Amy said, "OK, Chut. He's OK." The dog then dashed out to check the tires on the silver Porsche in the driveway.

"Come in. We're having coffee in the kitchen."

They walked side by side through Amy's wide center hall. Dort noted as they paused in the kitchen doorway that the chin of the thin, dark-haired man behind Amy was just a bit higher than the top of her head. Tim introduced himself again and, as the two men shook hands, Amy told him that Dort Adams was the local constable and one of the sheriff's deputies. Tim took the seat Dort pulled out and said, "I don't know where to begin."

"Begin with one of these." Dort held up the oatmeal cookie he was eating and, with his other hand, moved the blue-and-white jar down the table.

Tim looked from the cookie jar to Amy. "This is beautiful." His eyes moved to Dort's place at the table and a smile lit up his face. "With the cover intact. The last time I saw a ginger jar like this it was behind glass in a museum."

"My grandmother said this came from the Hilton side of the family. My great-grandmother Amy Hilton built this house in 1862, but I've no idea when that jar was brought to Maine.''

''I'm not trying to avoid the reason I'm here but old china and silver catch my attention.'' He turned to Amy. ''My grandmother Mozeson said the look on my face when I spotted old china was the same as the look women have when they see new babies. My parents didn't know what to make of my interest.''

Dort finished his cookie and his coffee, leaned back in the grandfather chair with its wide white oak arms, and said, ''We'd like to hear about last Sunday. Your father said you met the murder victim when you stopped at the restaurant on the turnpike, between Kittery and Portland.''

''Yes. We came out at the same time and he said he was looking for a ride to Route One and up to Thomaston. He was wearing a sweater but didn't have a jacket. He had no luggage except a knapsack, the kind of canvas bag students use to carry papers and notebooks on campus.''

Tim looked from Dort to Amy before he continued. ''He wasn't a talker. Maybe he had something on his mind. He didn't talk. Didn't even seem to look at the scenery. I'm not much for car chatter so that was all right with me. I didn't want idle chitchat. It wasn't until I paid the toll when I left the turnpike above Portland and told him we were headed for Route One that the kid said anything. He asked if I knew a town named Granton.''

Once again Tim Mozeson smiled. He looked at Amy and said, ''When I left my father's place, he was, as usual, wanting to be helpful but not knowing how. My dad is a nice person but he doesn't seem to have relating skills except in business matters. He's always been that way. As though he needs a clear path to a specific point or he's lost. No wandering, no exploring, no taking risks. I think he's afraid of living and after twenty-five years with my mother, that's not surprising. In her opinion, my father never did anything right. Except make money. But anyhow, as I was leaving, he gave me your name and address in case I needed any help while I was in Maine. It's the sort of thing my father does, has always done.''

Tim turned and spoke to Dort. "I only glanced at the paper Dad gave me but I noticed the name Granton because it was a Maine town I'd never heard of. So I told the boy I'd heard the name but knew nothing of the place. He said he was interested in family history and thought he might have some ancestors in a village called Granton. Said all he knew about it was that it was on a peninsula south of Rockland and there was a river running through it to the ocean at a place called Sacaja Harbor. I asked how he had tracked his relatives to this particular town. He patted his knapsack and said he'd found some papers. Then he laughed, a kind of hollow, unfunny laugh and said actually he had stolen the papers from the woman who called herself his mother.''

Dort leaned forward. "Hold it. Say that again.''

"What?''

"About his mother.''

"Oh, that. Odd, isn't it? He called her 'the woman who called herself my mother.'''

"So it wasn't necessarily distant ancestors he was looking for,'' Amy said. She glanced at Dort. She knew he had to be thinking the same thing.

"Go on,'' she said.

Tim held out his coffee mug and Dort refilled it. "I was in an antimother mood myself so I asked about his

father. He answered 'Him!' with disgust. I told him I'd
be turning off Route One before Wiscasset but could
drive him into that town if it would help. He said that
wasn't necessary. It was getting colder and starting to
rain when I let him out. That's when I suggested he take
the jacket. I had just tossed it into the car when I left
Ohio. It was a gift from my mother. I'd only worn it a
few times. My address was printed inside one pocket.
Grandmother Mozeson's custom. She came from Russia.
Relatives arriving in this country were located and identified because everyone's name was written inside a
pocket.''

They sat in silence, each processing what had been
said with what had been on their minds before. Amy
wanted to tell Tim to call his father and repeat what he'd
just told them—that he truly thought Sam Mozeson was
a fine man, a good man. That he'd always thought so.
She now had a lead toward answering the question that
had been gnawing at her since the moment she saw the
boy's face appear in the sawdust shed.

Dort said, ''You heard about the boy's death on radio
news?''

''The friends I'm staying with don't have TV and they
buy only the Sunday papers. I heard about it on my car
radio while driving into Bath to join them and some of
their friends for dinner. I left early and drove my own
car so I could browse in antique places—the few that
are open this month. The radio was on but, at first, I
didn't pay attention. Another murder. Then I heard the
name Granton followed by a state police bulletin about
trying to locate a Tim Mozeson who was driving a car
with Ohio license plates.''

Tim looked at Amy and shrugged his shoulders. ''My
first thought was that my name and a murder had gotten

garbled on the news network and my father was probably getting all sorts of screwy info. I don't have a car
phone. Never felt a need for one. So I stopped at the
first public phone I could find and called him. He told
me to come here. I don't know what set him off or
stirred him up but he was really upset. Didn't sound like
himself. He seemed to think you had some connections
with local law officers and could advise me on what to
do. My instinct was to call the state police immediately
but it seemed very important to my father that I talk to
you first. I've never done much to please him. My coming here seemed to matter to him. It was something I
could do. So here I am.''

"Amy found the body," Dort explained. "I'm the
local constable and a deputy so the sheriff asked for my
help. We've been sitting here trying to figure out what
we know and don't know. Your information is most welcome. I'll call the sheriff's office now before someone
notices your car in Amy's drive and thinks we're withholding evidence. Our sheriff was born in Massachusetts
and he's still learning that folks on this peninsula don't
always think the way he does. Amy, I don't think this
man has eaten. There's about one more serving of your
soup.''

"Soup and homemade bread, Tim?"

"I'd welcome food in any form. I didn't stop on the
way up because I wanted to get here before blue lights
told me to pull over. All the highway patrols must have
my license number now and there probably aren't too
many Ohio cars on Route One tonight.''

Amy heated the last of the *corba* in the microwave
and sliced a loaf of onion whole wheat bread. When she
set the food in front of Tim, he lifted the silver knife

with the twisted handle and said, "This I like. Old family silver?"

"Not my family. A gift. But they are old. They've been in use here on this peninsula for well over a hundred years. Not stuck in a drawer or wrapped in tarnish-proof cloth. Used and enjoyed every day. I've only had them a month but each day the heft and feel and look please me. Are you familiar with that design?"

Before Tim could answer, Chutney's barking was followed by a knocking on the front door. Dort hung up the phone and said, "I'll get it."

ELEVEN

BENTLEY WOODMAN had two men with him both wearing the brown uniforms of the sheriff's department. They followed Dort down the hall and into the kitchen. Tim stopped eating and stood to acknowledge introductions, then went back to his bowl of soup as though it might be snatched from him.

There was an uncomfortable moment of silence. Amy looked at the table, unconsciously counting chairs, wanting to start clearing away the dishes. Bent stood as straight as his five feet, eight inches allowed and the deputies, taller than their chief, remained in the background.

But Dort Adams, down-to-earth Dort, waved Bent over to the grandfather chair, carried off the dishes, and asked, "Which explanation do you want first?"

Bent Woodman sat back in the old chair, his hands on the wide arms, and looked from Dort to Amy. Tim buttered another slice of bread and watched Amy's face.

Woodman gestured toward Tim and asked, "Mrs. Creighton, how did you locate this man?"

"He found me," Amy said. "His father gave him my name and number when Tim said he was driving up to Maine. Sam Mozeson is the New York publisher I work for. I've never met Sam in person and never met Tim until he arrived here just a short time ago."

"Why did he come here instead of contacting my office or the state police? Where has he been?" Sheriff Woodman addressed his questions to Amy.

"Oh, fidgits. Double fidgits. Bentley Woodman, why are you questioning me when Tim Mozeson is right here, ready and willing to answer all your questions as soon as he finishes chewing that crust of bread? He was hungry and we fed him."

"We?" The sheriff didn't seem ready to deal with the situation that had brought him to this house.

The smell of fresh coffee filled the kitchen. Dort brought two chairs in from the hall, invited the deputies to sit at the long table, and asked Amy if there were more cookies. This was the ploy he had used years ago to divert the principal from noticing the equipment the high school boys had set up for the experiment that electrocuted the science lab's pet alligator. Offer food with friendly gestures. Dort had probably utilized this technique many times since he came back to live in Granton and became a constable.

"Coffee, Bent? Real cream." Dort took the refilled cookie jar from Amy, placed it in front of the sheriff, and moved the sugar and cream over beside the steaming mug of coffee. "Amy and I stayed at Doc Kelling's to talk with Alex Beaufort and see what Doc could tell us after his examination of the dog. By then we were both hungry. Amy had some food cooked. I didn't. So we're here. Now, you want to hear when Tim learned that he and his car were being sought and why he came here before calling you? Tim?"

Does hot soup dissolve tension? Amy glanced across the table at Tim. His thin face looked younger since he'd eaten. His tense, tight jaw line had relaxed almost into a smile.

"My father often treats me as though I'm twelve instead of thirty-two. I don't argue with him. Amy Creighton has been editing for my father for years and so, in case I might need adult advice while in the wilds of Maine, Dad gave me her name, address, and phone number. I humored him and put the card in my wallet. The friends I'm visiting on Westport Island don't have TV, don't read daily papers. So it wasn't until I turned on the car radio this evening on my way into Bath that I heard about the murder and that Maine law officers were trying to locate me and my car. I called my father so he'd know I was alive and well. He asked me to talk to Mrs. Creighton before calling the state police. Again, I humored him. My father was very upset and I couldn't see that another fifty minutes could make much difference."

"Here's an important point, Bent." Dort spoke before the sheriff could respond to Tim's words. "Tim told us that when he let Stillman out on Route One below Wiscasset Sunday night, the boy was carrying a knapsack, the kind of canvas bag college kids use for books or papers. No other luggage. Did your men find any such bag or papers when they searched the mill shed? In the sawdust or outside the building?"

Amy spoke up. "Some of the pussy willow shrubs in front of the sawdust shed were bent or broken. Did your men check those to see if a tractor or truck wheel might have caught and torn them? There's a trail or woods road behind the Morse Mill that's used by tractors. From the mill to East Granton. Had the mill staff used or seen anyone using that trail on Monday or Tuesday?"

Bentley Woodman sat straighter in the wide, old chair. Dort and Amy's diversionary tactics (informative but still diversionary) brought a change of expression to his face. The sheriff appeared more relaxed. He said, "I've heard stories about you two, in years past, combining your creative efforts to confuse Granton folks—mallard eggs slipped under brooding hens, an obituary in the Portland paper when Clarence Purdy's pig died, and something about ghosts that sailed on Sacaja Pond. My father told me about both of you. But I thought you gave up that behavior years ago."

"An obituary for a pig?" One of the deputies looked at Dort but the constable's face gave no clue to his thoughts.

It was Amy who said, "Philip Purdy. I liked the line in his death notice about his being greatly missed by all the neighbors. That monstrous boar kept getting loose. He ran wild all over Granton Hill, scared men, women, and children. He ate chickens and ducks, broke fences, and gobbled up every pumpkin for miles around. Philip Purdy was greatly missed. He really was. But Sheriff Woodman, Dort and I are only trying to add up what we know, what each of us has learned. We want to find out if our information meshes with what you've found out. We are not joking."

Dort asked, "What did the autopsy show?"

"Skull smashed. By a blow or the boy could have fallen on a rock. He was dead, had been dead for some time before he was carried into that shed." Woodman looked at his notepad. "Particles of clay on his pants and shoes. Lab is doing further tests on those. Last meal was cheese and crackers and milk. Eaten less than four hours before he died. No signs of a fight, a struggle. No bruises or broken nails. Hemlock cones in jacket pocket."

Woodman turned to Tim. "Could those hemlock

cones have been in your jacket when you loaned it to Stillman?''

"I'm sure I haven't worn that jacket since last fall," Tim said. "And I wouldn't know a hemlock cone if I saw one. Certainly never picked any. Were they fresh?"

"Yes. Tiny, new cones. At the stage where they look enameled.''

Dort watched the sheriff's face and then added another fact to the accumulating evidence. "Doc Kelling said the dog had clay particles on its skin. You might want to find out if they're the same as those found on the boy's clothing. We were thinking of materials carried in a pickup truck—cement, maybe clay from those old brick pits down at Sacaja Harbor."

Amy added, "The dog could have hopped into a truck, been an uninvited passenger. That's just a supposition but in case the clay particles are the same, the victim could have been at the harbor, could have been killed at the harbor. But any stranger walking around Sacaja Harbor or around Granton on a Monday in May would have been noticed. And that jacket was noticeable."

"You're right on that point," the sheriff said. "If Stillman was moving about anywhere in this area on Monday, someone would have noticed him, with or without that jacket. We need to know where he was between Sunday night and Monday night. But don't go wild with your speculations and suppositions. Don't ask me to believe the murderer was the same person who went in through the Fullerton root cellar, painted sixty-one pictures in that attic room, and then sat out on a windy hill Monday night with his headlights on the barn where that dog was chained up."

"Or camped out in one of those Sacaja Pond cabins

across from Hank Gustaffson's place," said Dort. "Did a search warrant help you find out what went on over there?"

"The owner says he gave his kids permission to camp out in that middle cabin. We have to accept his statement," Bent answered. "What we know is that four kids skipped school on Monday and drove up from Portland with lots of booze. No sign of drugs. None of them seems to have had brains enough to get a wood fire going. Their orgy wasn't so much fun when they all got cold. Several of them had regurgitation troubles. I hope the father who gave us that cover-up story makes those kids come up and clean the camp. But that mystery is solved."

Amy went down the hall to answer the beeping that signaled a call on her office phone. Sam Mozeson wanted to talk with Tim. When the phone in the kitchen rang, Dort rose to answer it. Alex Beaufort said he wanted the sheriff. There were prowlers outside his house.

"I'll ride with Dort," the sheriff told his deputies. "You go first. It's on Allen's Point Road where we checked on the broken windows last week. Last driveway on the river side. Look for a big white birch by the mailbox. Make a sharp right just before the mailbox. You'll go down a grade before you see the house. Turn on the flashing lights as you start down the drive. Not before."

TWELVE

THE RED SLASH in the darkness showed Amy the time was two a.m. Clocks should be round. Digital time looked like a neon sign on a roadhouse. And that, Amy Creighton told herself, dates you. You're getting old and set in your ways, opinionated, and....

Amy sat up in bed. What had awakened her? Chutney was curled up, sleeping quietly on her rug. She heard no sounds of rain or gusting winds. Amy slipped out of bed and into her robe—still the long, red, winter robe—and crossed to the window. Chutney rose and followed, rubbing against her thigh, silent except for her tail thumping against the dresser.

The bedroom windows overlooked the back lawn, sloping down to the brook. Amy's eyes, slowly picking out familiar shapes in the darkness, could see no deer standing or passing through. No movements. Had she been dreaming?

It had been almost midnight before she went to bed, after Tim Mozeson drove away. She'd offered him a room so he wouldn't be driving in the dark on unfamiliar roads, but he had declined. It was now Friday morning. The editing must be finished and the book mailed today and she'd told Tim she'd take him down to the harbor in the afternoon. Why? Because when he talked about old silver and china those tight lines in his face loosened.

Maybe his antique browsing and searching gave him the escape editing provided for her.

Escape? More than that, but working with words did offer an escape in the beginning. When her husband left, Amy needed something big enough, interesting and challenging enough, to occupy her mind. Something to help her feel competent and whole again. Yes, and a cash income earned without the emotional strain from being part of an office. No matter how sincerely concerned and caring her co-workers might be, Amy did not want to face questions every day about her broken marriage and her future plans. She wanted, needed, absorbing work, but work she could do alone.

She found more than escape. Through her editing for book publishers, Amy gained a renewal of the sense of self she had had growing up. "Don't argue with Amy." That admonition had been repeated over and over during her school years. Not because Amy Wainwright was arrogant and aggressive but because she enjoyed spending time finding answers, because she found learning exciting. Her father, Clark Wainwright, encouraged her curiosity and Amy grew up feeling uncomfortable with unanswered questions. She kept books moving back and forth between her rural mailbox and the Maine State Library, and, when she went to college, Amy Wainwright spent more time in the library than she did dating, dining, or dancing.

Selling off a few acres of the land Amy Hilton had bought back in the 1860s to add to her thirty acre dowry made it possible for Amy to have the larger back room in her home made into an office and to furnish it with what she needed. That sale also provided living expenses until she established a reputation with publishers and earned an adequate annual income. When she left her job in New York City and came back to Granton, she worked for the county newspaper. There she met and married Montgomery Creighton.

Monty shared Amy's pleasure in being outdoors—her reason for coming back to Granton—swimming, hiking, canoeing, and observing the daily changes on the land. They lived in the house her great-grandmother, Amy Hilton, had built during the Civil War. Until Monty met Charles Dunn and went with him to live in Arizona. An office in her home provided the isolation she needed at that time and editing was work she enjoyed.

The plan to drive down to Sacaja Harbor and introduce Tim Mozeson to Carrie Parker was made impulsively. Amy responded to the gulf between Tim's misery at his disappointing family relationships and his obvious pleasure in antique silver and china. She asked how he had learned about these, and when Tim talked about spending hours in New York libraries, hours haunting pawn shops, museums, and auction centers, Amy recalled her own youthful searches. She remembered moving away from friends and even from teachers who told her she was crazy. Told her she was foolish to waste time trying to find out things that were not important, digging for information that would bring neither cash nor public recognition.

So, late last night, Amy offered to take Tim down to Sacaja Harbor. She told him about Carrie Parker and her old china and silver, about Carrie's encyclopedic mind. Amy said she'd call ahead and arrange a visit for Friday afternoon and would, herself, be free after one p.m. An impulse. But it had been worth it to see the expression on the face of Sam's son.

Amy knew she needed more than two hours sleep but, now that she was fully awake, she also knew it would be better to get busy and finish editing the rest of the book rather than go back to bed and toss and turn. One advantage of living alone and being self-employed was setting her own schedules, shifting her hours when she wanted, or needed, to do so. She liked knowing no one would tell her she should be in bed when she felt like reading all night or getting up at four a.m. to make bread. Alone in her own home, no one bleated at her, ''What will the neighbors think?''

Three hours later the job was done. She'd take another look through her summary notes before driving to the post office, but the edited manuscript would go off by express mail as promised. Why had Sam specified Friday? This wasn't a book with any immediate time line. She knew that because she had edited it. Did Sam Mozeson spend lonely weekends with manuscripts?

But first breakfast and then the day was hers. Maybe she would make time to spread the sawdust that had been sitting in bags in her car since Wednesday morning. She could even check the asparagus bed before the morning invasion of the blood-sucking hordes of black flies. Amy mixed batter for apple-and-buckwheat muffins and put them in the oven. While these baked, she shifted a container of fish chowder and a quart of blackberries to the refrigerator and set a block of cheddar cheese out on the counter to soften to room temperature. She scrambled two eggs and they were ready when the timer buzzed.

Amy's breakfast reading this week was a book of essays written by a man who found gardening an individual step in remaining independent of the controlling, greedy commercial world. She had driven up to Thomaston and bought a copy after she found herself starting to highlight and underline the author's ideas in the

Granton library copy of the book. Since she started to
read and borrow books, librarians had chided her about
this habit. They called it defacing books. But, in Amy's
view, marking lines and phrases made them easier to
remember, made it easier to find again to ponder. The
author of these essays raised garlic in New Mexico. Amy
grew vegetables and fruits in Maine. Both Amy and the
author had found that ties to the soil gave them a sense
of being in control of their lives, of being independent.

Chutney was waiting by the back steps and went hur-
tling down to the brook and then back, yelping with
pleasure when she found Amy was going to keep her
company during this morning's woods patrol. They followed the path west, along the brook, and crossed on
the log bridge. Amy pushed at several of the upright
posts and found they had rotted at the base. These would
need to be replaced before the bridge weakened.

The path curved down around a mass of boulders to
Amy's sandy beach on Ward's Pond. Further east of this
cove, and along both sides of the pond, there were now
dozens of summer cottages. Aside from having a few
trees cut to let the summer sun warm the beach and the
cove, Amy's shore hadn't changed much since Joshua
Hilton deeded it to his daughter in 1859 and she had had
lumber cut to build herself a house and a barn. In the
last part of the twentieth century, before the summer
folks arrived, opened their camps and burned gasoline
racing boats up and down the pond, and after they left
in September, this beach was secluded enough for swimming without a suit, a pleasure Amy had enjoyed since
she learned to swim in this cove at age seven.

Chutney dashed into the pond and swam around in
circles. Amy took off her sneakers and waded. In another
week the water would be warm enough for a brisk swim.

Chutney paddled out of sight behind the big, rounded boulder Amy's father had called "the whale." During high school days, she and Dort had tried to out-swim each other around and around that great, gray rock. Returning hot and sweaty from their hikes through the valley, they often plunged into the pond without removing even their sneakers.

As she sat on the rocks above the beach putting her sneakers back on, Amy felt that tingle alerting her again, telling her she was almost remembering something. She sat motionless looking at her footprints in the wet sand. Footprints. Handprints. Fingerprints. Foot, hand, finger, thumb. What else had she seen Wednesday morning when the sliding sawdust revealed a shoulder, then an ear and a cheek, then an arm and a hand, when the body had been exposed in the mill shed?

Amy had told Dort she had a feeling she knew something she didn't know she knew. What was there about that scene in the Morse Mill sawdust shed that felt familiar, that hung on the edges of her mind?

THIRTEEN

THE ALARM SOUNDED at ten-thirty a.m. Amy switched it off and sat on the edge of the bed, orienting herself and sorting out uneasy feelings—dreams of fire trucks, nagging but evasive thoughts and the strangeness of awakening to bright sunlight. She had intended to sleep for a short time and then get out to mulch her strawberries. Now that would have to wait until tomorrow. Today's priority was to get the manuscript to the post office.

The editing was done. Even if she took more than thirty minutes to check her summary notes, she'd still have time to drive to the village and be back before Tim Mozeson came. Amy wondered briefly what professional freelance editors wear on business trips and what Carrie and Jeb Parker and others of their generation expected middle-age women to wear. But she made her decision in favor of comfort, dressing in clothes that would allow her to show Tim the walks along the rocky shore. Blue jeans (the new ones), a soft rose turtleneck and a deeper rose sweater. And sneakers (also new) with grip soles for climbing across ledges and surf-washed rocks. As she passed the hall mirror, Amy thought her attire could be classified as ''work clothes,'' as most uniforms are, to accommodate hours in her office with side trips to the garden.

She took time for a cup of coffee, a muffin, and a

slice of cheese but didn't switch on the phone answering machine although it was blinking. She needed an uncluttered mind to review her notes.

The Granton post office, set twenty feet back from the sidewalk, had benches facing each other across what the villagers called Hollyhock Square. Years ago, a retired carpenter built four benches to be used by folks waiting for the mail or stopping to socialize on daily trips to the post office. Ted Marston, who was postmaster then, hauled in soil to make flower beds between the property line fences and the benches and planted hollyhocks. Gardeners on the peninsula and summer folks supplied seeds for better and brighter hollyhocks. Plants with pale or dull flowers were removed, leaving those with bright or deeply colored blossoms. Bees mixed the pollens. Every year in late August, ripe seed pods were snipped from the post office plants and passed around. Granton hollyhocks, one of the joys of the summer season, now grew in almost every dooryard for miles around. On this May morning, luxuriant hollyhock leaves in the beds behind the benches spread and reached for the sun.

There was a nether side to Hollyhock Square. The women and girls in Granton often called that twenty-foot walkway between the two sets of benches "The Gauntlet." The men of the village and surrounding areas seemed to be the ones with time to sit and chat—and to make comments about those coming and going. Most of the time the remarks were friendly, even humorous. But some tongues had cutting edges.

Amy didn't look to see who was holding down the benches when she carried her package into the post office shortly before noon. She waved and called out a cheerful "Good morning" to both sides as she hurried inside. While she was filling out the express mail forms,

Charlie Benton moved over to the counter beside her and said, "Hear you and Dort Adams is solving a murder. How long you two been back together?"

Amy, focused on completing weeks of work, finished signing the forms and paid the postmaster before she turned to Charlie, who was repeating his question. With the book off to New York, Amy felt she had closed one door and was free to open another. "Sorry, Charlie. Were you speaking to me?"

"You know damn well I was. You don't notice ordinary folks, do you?"

Charlie was the last of the local Bentons. And thanks for that, Amy thought as she backed away from the old man. This Benton was known as a pillar of the church—probably more for his cash contributions than his good works. Old Charlie's righteous howling, at town meetings and any other places where something stirred him up, was offset by his malicious gossiping. Charlie Benton had wagged a wicked tongue as long as Amy had known him.

"Business matters, Charlie," Amy said. "I had to get that book off in the mail today. You had a question?"

"You and Dort Adams spending time together?"

"Dort's our local constable. I've been talking with him and with Sheriff Woodman. I had to—I found the body, you know." Amy turned back to the postmaster. "Thanks, Jim. I'll be back next week for another package."

Two of the men sitting on the benches stood up when Amy came out. Arthur Waldron nodded. His cousin Stanley asked, "What's the sheriff found out about that murder? We saw his car at your house last night."

Amy looked from Stanley to Arthur and back again. Why would either of these Waldron men have been driving past the lane to her house last night or any other night? Her house wasn't on a direct way to or from anywhere and, from the public town road, no one could look around the curve in the drive or through the hedges and see a car. Not even the sheriff's car. Why had these two been watching her house?

"You've probably heard everything I've heard," Amy answered. "Maybe more. I haven't listened to either the radio or TV this morning. What's the latest report?" This was a tactic her father, Clark Wainwright, had taught her—turn unwelcome questions back to the nosy questioners.

Arthur stooped to pat the old calico cat sunning herself on a post office bench. Stanley looked over Amy's shoulder. Did Stanley Waldron ever make eye contact with anyone? With his wife or his boss? With his cousin Arthur?

"Portland station said the guy was dead before his body was put in that shed." The Wainwright tactic had worked. Stanley answered her question. "Said the murdered guy came from New York State, was looking for his family in Granton. You ever hear of a Stillman family around here?"

"Did they say family or ancestors?"

"Family, I think. What's the difference? You know any Stillmans in these parts?"

Amy looked at both men and wondered why they were here in town at this hour on Friday instead of being at work. Arthur was dressed for the office, his insurance office in East Granton, neat in a fussy gray suit, blue shirt, dark tie, and polished black shoes. Stanley's boots were muddy. Under his faded flannel shirt he wore a ragged T-shirt promoting beer and the ribs were worn from the thigh sections of his corduroy pants. From lifting and moving sacks and boxes at the orchard where he worked?

"Ancestors could have different names," Amy said. "The maiden names of all the mothers and their parents." Amy looked up at Stanley, whose eyes were still focused on the white picket fence behind her. She glanced over at Arthur, but he kept his attention on the cat. There were lots of Waldrons around Granton and throughout the county. Old Will Waldron, the one with the terrible temper, had had five or six sons and so had his brother over Waldoboro way.

"You two are cousins," Amy said. "But your mothers had different names and so did your grandmothers. Didn't one of you have a grandmother who was a Parker?"

The two men looked at each other briefly and then at Amy but, before either one could reply, Charlie Benton shuffled out into the sunny square and demanded Arthur's attention. They attended the same fundamentalist church in East Granton.

As Amy crossed the street to her car, she wondered if Stanley Waldron had been inside a church since his mother's funeral, when he was a child. Had he developed that shifty-eyed habit in reform school, or in the house of correction, or whatever it was called in those days, the place he'd been sent for butchering Paul Fullerton's steers and peddling the beef in Augusta? That was more than twenty years ago. But in Granton, people's pasts were not forgotten. When Julia Carmody died last month at the age of ninety-three, someone attending the funeral service mentioned that Julia "had to get married" when she was fifteen. And the day Ruel Griffin's casket came home to Granton for committal services and his eighty-eight-year-old body was buried beside his three wives, there were remarks about Seth, the son Ruel had acknowledged and supported but whose mother had not been one of his legal wives.

Amy looked back at the post office and watched Emma Waldron, Arthur's wife, approach the three men, moving in with the thrust of an ocean liner steaming into a fishing cove. Charlie Benton and Stanley Waldron were as tall as Emma but her bulk and posture diminished both of them. As Amy looked at Emma standing beside Arthur, she thought of an article she'd read recently about praying mantises—the large, dominant female and the smaller, wily, quick-moving male, seeking ways to satisfy his wants. And then another image stirred Amy to a quiet chortle. A private game she and Dort had played years ago.

When they were both home in Granton during the summers of their college years, they observed local couples and speculated on their love-making practices. Was it physically possible for good Deacon Fowler and his wife, both weighing more than two hundred and fifty pounds, to utilize the missionary position? Did raunchy old Bill Ginnis ever imitate the heated behavior of the hound dogs he bred? How would Dort Adams respond today if she asked him to visualize the bedroom behavior of Arthur and Emma Waldron?

Her thoughts shifted again. Were there other Granton people, besides Doc Kelling and nasty-minded old Charlie Benton, noticing and commenting on the fact that Dort Adams and Amy Creighton were spending hours together this week? No one had ever come right out and asked Amy why she and Dort, who had been a "couple" from junior high days through high school and beyond their college graduations, had left town the same month, going off to different destinations.

Both had returned to Granton after working in other states and in the thirty years since then, both had married and then divorced after their spouses left them. No one asked Amy why she and Dort never resumed any kind of relationship. She knew that in this small Maine town, although no one asked, folks did wonder why Amy and Dort were never seen to exchange more than casual greetings. Until this week.

It had been pure chance that Dort Adams was the first person Amy bumped into Wednesday morning after she found the body. She asked him for help because he was the town constable, the local law officer, and knew the proper procedures. But the two of them had slipped into a number of old, almost forgotten patterns of relating as, together, they brought up and laid out questions and theories about the murder.

Amy looked in the rearview mirror of her hatchback and watched the townspeople cross the common to the post office. She had lifted out the seventh bag of sawdust because it hindered her driving view. Maybe seeing it each time she entered the garage would help her get at the process of spreading this mulch. But not this afternoon.

On the drive back to her house, Amy went back over her encounter with Dort on the mill steps and over the past two days and admitted that she was enjoying his company. Some of the relating patterns were comfortable and pleasant. The years, the old hurts and misunderstandings, faded as they ate together again at her old oak table, bouncing speculations off each other. And...

Yes, it was true. Amy was pleased to find that she and Dort were able, once again, to communicate without words.

FOURTEEN

AMY TURNED ON her answering machine as soon as she came into the house to find a series of messages. Polly Anderson's whining voice complained about those awful foreign people hired to work in fast food stores, taking jobs away from good Americans but, primarily, she wanted news about that awful murder.

Carrie Parker, after stating that she did not like to talk to machines, asked if Amy would stop at Morse Mill on the way to the harbor and bring down the hinges her husband had ordered.

Ruth Waldron, speaking for herself, and not because Doc Kelling asked her to call, said that Alex Beaufort had decided he didn't want to keep his dog. Did Amy know of a good home? Margaret was a loveable animal.

Dort's message began to replay just as he stepped up to the kitchen door with Chutney circling his legs and whimpering with pleasure. He had called an hour ago to ask when Amy would be free to talk.

"Come through to the back, Dort. We can talk while I stretch. I'm full of knots."

"My boots are muddy," he said. "I'll walk around on the lawn. Come on, Chut."

Amy hung from her exercise bar and stretched her toes down, one foot at a time. Dort sat on the bench beside the budding lilacs. Chutney dashed back and forth between them. "Dort, I was just talking with Stanley and Arthur Waldron in front of the post office. Well, actually, Arthur didn't open his mouth, but the two of them were together. Stanley told me they saw the sheriff's car here last night. How? You can't see my house from the road. You can't see my house or the area where your truck and the sheriff's car were parked. And even if you could, what were Stanley and Arthur Waldron doing out here on Hilton Road at that time of night?"

"That's what Bent would like to know. But he didn't know whose car it was. When the deputies went barreling out of your lane last night, they almost hit a car parked across the road. No lights. By the time Bent and I came out, that car was driving down the road, heading toward East Granton. We didn't know that car or any car had been parked without lights, across from your lane, until after we'd settled old Beaufort."

"Did he have prowlers?"

"Coons. Four big ones. Beaufort is not a country person. When the deputies focused the spotlight on the invaders, two of the coons sat up and snarled and looked mean. I think poor Alex was ready to head for Route One and a nice safe motel."

"I don't know whether you heard Ruth Waldron's message on the machine. It was personal—her thoughts, not Doc Kelling's. Beaufort doesn't want Margaret anymore. I think Ruth hopes one of us will take her." Amy stretched her toes again, moved to the stool, and down to the porch. She shook out her arms. "Maybe if the dog's name was Maggie or Mag, the poor beast would have a better chance of finding a good home."

"You may be right. What I came to ask you about is the name Stillman. Does it ring any bells, trigger any thoughts or connections? Can you recall coming across that name at any time around here? The Maine state police have the cooperation of the state police in New York but William Stillman's parents are behaving like nut cases. They sound as though they think someone should have stopped their son from messing up their lives by coming up to Maine and getting himself murdered. Makes me wonder how they treated the kid when he was little. Adds veracity to his story about wanting to find some family connections here. The Stillmans are sending an attorney to handle what needs handling.''

Amy's response was quick. "That's wicked and evil and awful. You mean neither his mother nor his father wants to be here, wants to find out what happened to their own child?''

"They both told the police that William Stillman is not their child. They adopted him. Sounds as though they abandoned him some time back.''

"Are you telling me they adopted him in Maine? In this part of Maine?''

Chutney's barking reminded Amy that Tim was due. She asked Dort to go around to meet him while she locked up. She made a comfort stop before she picked up the book of poetry for Carrie and a bag of cheese and cookies to nibble on at the shore. There were many things she still wanted to ask Dort, but a look at Tim's smiling face settled the question of what was top priority for this afternoon.

"Dort, I'm having fish chowder tonight. Could we do a catch-up over supper?''

"Fine. I'll stop at Doc Kelling's and see Margaret this afternoon, find out what he feels should be done with the dog.''

The strong pine odor from the bags of sawdust still waiting to be unloaded reproached her for her slothfulness earlier that morning, but Amy turned her thoughts to showing Tim her home territory. When they crossed the bridge over Ward's Pond Stream, Amy told Tim that the stream flowed into Sacaja Pond. Their drive would follow the Sacaja River, a much larger stream that flowed down through the peninsula, through Sacaja Pond, and then into the ocean at the harbor.

Carrie's package was ready at the Morse Mill office. As Amy came out of the mill driveway and turned south, she stopped in front of Ira Bellhouse's small brown house so Tim could look across to see the open-sided shed where she found the body on Wednesday morning.

"The sheriff told me someone carried him in there after he was dead," Tim said. "I couldn't have lifted him. Wouldn't it take two people to carry someone his size up into that shed?"

"Depends on the man. What he lifts in his daily routines," Amy said.

"Why there? Why in that building? It's so open. Wouldn't a car or truck parked in that drive at night be noticed?"

"There's not much traffic on this road at night in May," Amy answered. "If headlights caught a reflection of a shiny bumper, glass in a taillight, fancy spoke wheels or such, a driver might wonder why someone was there. The state police have put out several bulletins asking for information."

It was eight miles from Morse Mill to the harbor and Tim was free to turn and look in all directions, to note stone walls, old white houses with dark shutters, and lush green fields sloping down to the widening river. Along one wooded stretch, Amy stopped the car and lifted hemlock boughs to show Tim tiny, perfect hemlock cones—the kind the staff at the state lab found in the pocket of the jacket Stillman was wearing.

Sacaja Harbor was built in layers. On the spine of the headland, the town businesses faced each other across the end of the state road. To get down to the town wharf and the docks used by the fishermen, one could follow the switchbacks along the east side of the bluff or take the steep road down to the west.

Amy chose to drive down the steep hill and circle around past the shacks and sheds of the fishermen, past the marina service buildings and the wharf where the Bean Island mailboat docked. She wanted Tim to get his first sight of Carrie and Jeb Parker's house looking up at it from the harbor.

"Let's get out for a moment," Amy said. "Then you can smell the salt air and hear the gulls and the surf, feel how different this is from Cincinnati and the Ohio River. I want to breathe a bit of ocean air.

"The first settlers here built up on the headland where the post office, the store, and the inn are now." Amy pointed in that direction. "They feared night vapors from the water—believed they held a miasma that caused fevers and weakness. The settlers who went up river to Granton and beyond built their homes away from the river for the same reason."

Amy pointed toward the houses on the road curving down to the east from the village center. "The last Cape Cod house over there, the low white one with the hemlock hedge behind it, is Carrie Parker's. Built by Captain Philip Parker in 1796. From his front parlor he looked down on his docks and his ships. Carrie was born in that house. Born a Parker and married a Parker, a third cousin. Let's go up."

FIFTEEN

CARRIE PARKER came around from behind the shed as Tim and Amy drove in. She waved the blue enamel bucket she was holding and said, "Buried my compost. You'd think after doing that for eighty years the backyard would be higher than the house. Hungry bacteria in this coastal soil."

Carrie's corduroy skirt and flannel shirt had faded to the same dull blue but her new cotton sweater was a ripe eggplant purple. "You're looking well, Amy. This must be the young man who likes old silver and china."

"Carrie Parker, this is Tim Mozeson. I've told him about some of the dishes you've shown me. Perhaps I've overdone it but I'm enjoying Tim's anticipation."

Tim stood behind Amy on the crushed shell path and acknowledged the introduction to the tall woman who waited, holding the shed door open. Carrie Parker had a regal quality, accentuated by her height and her gray hair neatly held in a French twist, but her smile and voice were warm and welcoming.

"As long as you're not one of those cheap, persistent buyers with no manners, you can look and rave all you want." Carrie led the way to the kitchen and waved Tim on through to her sitting room where she had china pieces set out on the long harvest table under the front windows. "The last fellow who wanted to buy old stuff out of my attic talked at me as though he thought anyone living in this village must be missing brain power, lacking sense equal to his. And he called me 'dearie.' That's when I shut the door in his face.''

Amy watched Tim as he stepped into the next room and moved toward a table, quietly, almost reverently, a young man with a glow about him. This is what Sam Mozeson needed to see and understand. Surely Sam would feel differently toward the son he spoke of as a stranger if he saw him now, alive with excitement and anticipation, happy in a field that had meaning for him.

''Let me rinse out this pail and wash my hands.'' Carrie crossed to the slate sink that stretched for five feet along the back wall of the kitchen. The rich, polished sink shelves and the high back were spotless, smooth and black—smoother, perhaps, than the day those slate pieces had been assembled in this coastal kitchen. Were any other such sinks still in use in homes here at the harbor? This one was not only an antique, it was an aesthetic delight. A museum piece.

The year the Parkers decided to have water from their spring piped down into the house, one of the Parker daughters was being courted by a young man whose family was making money supplying settlers and lumber camps up in the Moosehead area of Maine. Profits accumulated with each wagonload hauled up to Greenville—food, boots, tools, grain for the horses and oxen, and rum for Saturday nights.

This affluent suitor had a cousin who was gambling on another money-making venture—slate from the Monson hills. The wagons that hauled supplies up to Moosehead carried slate on their way back down to the coast. Sinks, fireplace panels and hearths, gravestones, and foyer floors were crafted from Monson slate by local stonecutters. High quality products went into the homes of local sea captains and sailed off with those captains for profitable sales in Boston and New York.

The beautiful sink in Carrie Parker's kitchen was made during that courtship summer. The Parker family was having water piped into the house. The suitor from Moosehead brought his slate dealing cousin to the harbor to talk with a group of stonecutters, recent arrivals from Finland. The craftsmen demonstrated their skills by creating and installing this great stone sink, still in use today. The stone cutters and fitters met all the requests of the Parker wife—a sink long enough to hold a milk can for thorough washing, deep enough to bathe the children, and high enough in back to keep splashes off the wall.

"I wish Amy Hilton had put in a slate sink when she built her house—my house," Amy said. "Yours is beautiful."

"She built during the Civil War. Her options were limited," Carrie said. "Later, when there was money and materials, your grandmother Katherine wanted windows. She wanted light more than she wanted a slate sink. She wanted windows above the sink that was there and windows beside the table where they ate so she could look down to the brook. The carpenters thought they could manipulate a widow lady and told her windows in that wall would spoil the symmetry or such. Told her windows couldn't be put in that wall because of bearing timbers and support beams. Those men didn't know Katherine—didn't know she had managed the ranch in Utah during the years her husband was dying. She shooed those Waldron workmen out of her house and hired carpenters from over Warren way. Clint Waldron stayed mad at your grandmother and her family as long as he lived."

"I remember old Will Waldron and his terrible temper. He never seemed to have much logic or reason on his side. Do all the Waldrons have such tempers? Stay mad for years?"

"You can't say 'all the Waldrons' anymore than you can say all the cats or all the dogs. But the Waldron men around here do seem to stick together, especially when it's a case of being 'against' something or somebody. But I like to think that through the years some of that nastiness has been bred out of them. Two Parker women married Waldrons, back about eighty years ago. I remember Jenny Waldron bringing her baby to a family picnic here when I was a girl. I was maybe six or seven and she let me hold and rock the little fellow."

"Mrs. Parker?" Tim stood in the doorway holding a deep octagonal-shaped dish, white inside but with a rich blue and white pattern on the outside and on the wide lip. "Do you know where this came from? Any history on this piece?"

"That dish isn't from my family. I do have a pitcher and a sugar bowl in that pattern that my grandmother found out on Bean Island after a house burned there." Carrie took the dish and held it out to Amy.

"This one, I call it a vegetable dish, I bought about twenty years ago from a family that was moving. They were trying to raise cash. I also bought some books and a roll of tarnish-proof cloth with nine silver forks in it. They hadn't lived here long and I never knew why they were in such a hurry to leave or where they went."

Carrie looked from Tim to Amy. "Odd. I hadn't looked at this serving dish in years. It's not one I display because the cover's missing. But I know the pattern is really old so I brought it out this morning for your friend to see. Holding it reminded me of the couple who sold it to me. I hadn't thought of them for years but, when I looked at this old blue design, I remembered the day I bought it. Their name was the same as that young man who was murdered—Stillman.''

SIXTEEN

AMY HAD TO LOOK in the phone book to find Dort's home number. When he didn't answer, she dialed the sheriff's office but the man on the desk couldn't or wouldn't tell her where she could reach either Bent or Dort. Amy made sure the answering officer had her name right and could read Carrie's number back to her correctly. Then she said, "Please contact Dort Adams or Sheriff Woodman on their car phones. Have one of them call me here. Tell them I have information on the Stillman family, information relating to the Stillman murder."

When Amy turned away from the phone, Tim and Carrie's husband, Jeb, were seated side by side at the kitchen table, munching molasses cookies. Carrie was pouring coffee into beautiful, large blue-and-white cups. "If that Stillman couple adopted a baby here in this town or county, wouldn't the adoption record be in the courthouse?" Carrie asked. She had been mulling over the facts Amy had told her, the reasons the sheriff and state police were tracking information on Stillman families.

"The sheriff can check the court records," Amy said. "But why would a couple with a new baby be in a hurry to leave town? If it was a trust fund baby, why move away?"

"That's one I've never heard before," Tim said.

"What is a trust fund baby? Is that a Maine phrase or a local one?"

Jeb chuckled. "You've heard the expression 'more money than brains'? And the one describing young men as having 'the morals of a Tom cat'? Around here those sayings often go together. They're used to explain the way some wealthy families settled the results of their sons' summer escapades—by setting up trust funds. The tangible results of a lusty summer were not totally abandoned. The little ones, the annual crop of bastard babies, were provided for. Never acknowledged, but the kids could be fed. One fund put a boy through Harvard. Maybe the Stillmans were paid to adopt a baby and take it out of town. Carrie, can you think of other reasons why a couple with a new baby might suddenly leave town?"

"Who said it was a new baby?" Carrie asked.

"You told us you thought it was 'about' twenty years ago when you bought the dish and forks," Amy said. "Can you be more specific? What else was going on at the time?"

Carrie looked at Jeb. "We had the green Plymouth then. I remember noticing the Stillman's car because it was parked beside ours, out there in the driveway, and I remarked that the colors were the same. When did we trade that one?"

"Didn't trade it," Jeb said. "Sold it to Jesse Perkins's boy when we bought Judge Morton's Pontiac. Remember? The judge died in October and his nephew came up from Philadelphia to settle the estate. That Pontiac would have been a good buy except about that time the price of gas went up. The judge's big car used twice as much gas as our little Plymouth."

"Amy, you said Sheriff Woodman checked the boy's

college records so he must have his birth date." Carrie held her cup with both hands as though her fingers needed warming. "The baby the Stillmans adopted might have been a year old. If they were paid to take a baby and move out of state, there must have been something about the child that could have connected that particular baby to somebody, some family in this area."

Carrie smiled at Tim. "We have our local soap operas. About thirty years ago, Judge Morton wrote an article for the paper—local history with a bit of genealogy. He mentioned an island family with webbed toes. In every generation of the Hendersons, most of the males had an extra flap of skin between two of their toes. About a month after that story was printed, a harbor fisherman drowned and when his body was found and brought in, a reporter noted the man had webbed toes. Mentioned it in his newspaper story. It stirred gossip and speculation from here to Augusta. Folks counted back, trying to recall which members of that island family were courting or such nine months before that fisherman was born. Kept tongues wagging for weeks."

"Did anyone find a connection to the islanders?" Tim asked.

Jeb answered. "Yes. It was too bad. Shook up a lot of families and it never should have happened. Probably the only time in his life Len Henderson touched a woman other than his wife. He was sixty years old. High seas had kept him on the mainland for three nights, couldn't cross to the island. He stayed down here at the harbor in one of the fish houses. One night Sally Vincent came in there to hide. Her husband was drunk and mean. Henderson had a fire going but those fish shacks are mighty drafty. They probably huddled together to keep warm. Len never knew about Sally's baby. No one would ever have known if Pat Vincent hadn't drowned and Sally, who'd just been saved, thought God was punishing her and confessed her sin. I think she sinned more by confession and messing up a lot of lives than she did by one night of responding to human comfort in a cold harbor fish house.''

Amy frowned as she listened to Jeb's tale of the webbed toes. She turned back to Carrie. ''Do you remember what Stillman did? Where he worked, for whom? Can you recall where they lived? You said it was at the harbor.''

''They lived on Allen's Point Road. Stanley Waldron owns the house now. Bought it from his aunt after he came back from serving time for his butchering. Must have squirreled away some of that meat money. Stillman did books for Morse Mill. Did taxes for some lobstermen and island folks.'' Carrie turned to Jeb. ''Was Stillman the name that came up this spring when someone on Bean Island was mixed up in a tax fraud case? Something to do with cheating summer folks. Or am I thinking of the time Courtney Cameron died and the police swarmed all over the harbor and the islands for weeks because his family insisted bonds were missing? That was a long time ago.''

''Courtney Cameron. I remember that name,'' Amy said. ''My father called him the Puritan patriarch. None of his children dared to dispute him and they came when he called. Didn't he die on Bean Island?''

''Another case of weather control. The seas were too high for Cameron's boat to take his housekeeper back to the island. The old man died alone.'' Jeb spread his hands in a gesture expressing futility. ''Courtney Cameron had millions, more money than one family could ever spend, but he had no one to hold his hand as he left this life. No questions about his death. He was ninety-four. He just stopped breathing and slipped away, sitting in his chair, watching the storm. Then his children began fighting over the estate. Claimed someone had taken bonds from the safe in the island home. Case never was solved.''

Jeb rose to answer the phone. Amy reached for the receiver before he said, ''It's for you. Sheriff Woodman.''

SEVENTEEN

THE SHERIFF WAS brief and brisk. He asked Amy to drive up to Allen's Point Road. He'd meet her there in ten minutes.

Amy's years working for newspapers set off warning signals and triggered questions. But Bentley Woodman's tone of voice and the specific time he set convinced her to follow his request and ask questions later. Had he received her phone message? Or had Dort told him she would be at Carrie Parker's house?

She told the Parkers and Tim what the sheriff wanted and said she didn't think she'd be gone long. To Carrie she added, "Tim is too courteous to interrupt but I know he's hoping you'll show him some of your old silver. Are the forks you bought from the Stillmans handy-by? Tim might recognize the design. I'm thinking about clues in everything. Probably you already know the history of the pattern on that silver."

Allen's Point Road turned west from the harbor road about two miles north of Sacaja. When settlers built on the point before 1800, water was the highway. Folks traveled by boat up river and along the coast. During the past forty years, titles to many old salt water farms had changed hands. Local owners, folks getting older, sold to real estate brokers. A few old houses were restored and additions built to make room for grandchildren and guests. But most of the fishermen's farmhouses and barns were knocked down and replaced by ten-room cottages with three-car garages.

Amy parked in the turn-out built to accommodate trucks carrying lumber to build those summer cottages and, according to information in the local papers, to show taxpayers how their dollars were being spent. These spaces at crossroads were needed so that school buses, fire trucks, and ambulances could turn.

During their high school years when she and Dort rode their bicycles down here on exploring trips, this had been a rutted, hump-centered one-lane road. The summer before she left for college, Amy drove her father's car and one day, here at this turn, she and Dort argued about driving the car out to the point on this humped-up road. That summer they argued about everything. Even food. Both of them brought lunch that day for their Allen's Point picnic. Amy smiled, remembering. They had eaten every crumb.

She and her husband hadn't argued. Monty wouldn't. Maybe in those years he couldn't. Amy thought of lukewarm milk—an ocean of tepid, unruffled whiteness. With a top layer of smooth oily cream. Why had she given up so easily after Monty first left? Why hadn't she tried other ways of relating, a middle ground between constant disagreements, exciting emotionally charged arguments and that deadly, passive, smothering blandness?

She used effective relating skills in her work. *Yes, Amy Creighton,* she told herself, *in professional and business relationships, a person can stand back, maintain safe or comfortable distances.* Who thinks of distances, safe or otherwise, in moments like those she had been vividly reminded of by that October painting in the Fullerton attic?

Bent Woodman braked the sheriff's department car beside Amy's compact and said, "Ride with me."

Allen's Point Road wasn't paved but cottage owners paid to have good gravel spread after the town crew did the April grading. Amy and Bent passed roads built as driveways to summer cottages, two neatly landscaped mobile homes, and then, on the right, the old gray house Carrie said the Stillmans had lived in. Stanley Waldron's house now. Before Amy mentioned this, the sheriff spoke.

"Beaufort's got prowlers on the brain. State lab report came in. The clay Doc Kelling found on that dog is the same as that on Stillman's clothes so Dort came down to have a look around the point in daylight. On the way, he picked up Beaufort's dog. Said he wanted to see if watching the dog wander loose would give him an idea of where the dog usually went. Some such notion.

"Dort told me he and the dog went out to the point and walked back along the shore. But when they came up over the rocks in front of Beaufort's cottage, that fool man blasted at them with a shotgun. Fortunately, he knows next to nothing about guns or buckshot. But some pellets hit the dog. Dort smashed the gun, swore at Beaufort, and then got his truck and took the animal back to Doc Kelling's. Called me on the car phone. Dort has a theory that Beaufort is afraid of men, sees them as authority figures, is used to being bossed by women. He thought you might be able to talk to the man. Calm him down so we can find out what's bugging him."

Bent turned on his flashing lights as he made the sharp turn down Beaufort's driveway and almost hit the pickup truck starting up the grade. Stanley Waldron backed down, gave the sheriff room to drive in, then headed up and out before Woodman could do more than lift his hand. "What's eating him? Doesn't that guy ever stay at his job?"

"Where does he work?" Amy asked.

"Finley's Orchards, up by Route One. If he hasn't been fired. I don't know why anyone would want to have such a mean-mouthed, surly guy around no matter how good a tree pruner he may be. Sorry, Amy, but that's one person I can't like."

Alex Beaufort came out of his garage. Had he been about to follow Waldron?

Bent and Amy both stepped out of the car, but, before the sheriff could move away from the door on his side, Amy reached out. With her hand firmly on Beaufort's shoulder, she asked, "Are you all right? You're shaking. Where's your jacket?"

Alex Beaufort turned back into the garage, pulled a green-and-black fleece jacket from his car, and slipped his arms into it. "Come inside," he said. "I need to sit down."

They followed him in. The large room on the ocean side of this new cottage was splendid in size and light but the furnishings were a mismatched jumble. The chairs and couches appeared to be castoffs from several cottages, not ugly but nondescript and dull. Windows filled the walls on three sides. Those on the left provided a view along the shore to the high rocks at the tip of the point. From the windows on the right, one could see along the wooded edge of the north side of this peninsular bulge to the curve of beach and fence that marked the boundary of Beaufort's property. Anyone fretting about prowlers around here had, on the water side, almost a lookout or tower view. If Beaufort had been looking for prowlers from this room, he would have seen Dort and the dog walking the shore toward his house.

Sheriff Woodman appeared to entertain similar thoughts. He crossed from the north windows to those with an unobstructed view out to the point, the shoreline where Dort and the dog had walked, approaching this cottage. Without turning from the window, Bent asked, "Was Stanley Waldron here when you shot your dog?"

"No. Mr. Waldron drove in after Mr. Adams left. He said he was looking for a bag he lost last week when he was down here." Mr. Adams? Where had this man been socialized? Beaufort huddled in his jacket although the room was warmed by the afternoon sun and by an operating furnace.

"Why was Stan Waldron down here last week?" Bent asked.

"I don't know. I didn't ask him and he didn't say. His house is just up the road." Alex Beaufort was rattled. Was he afraid of Stanley Waldron?

Amy made eye contact and spoke softly. "Alex, you've reported prowlers disturbing you. You've called the sheriff's office twice." She sat down and settled into a big, fan-back wicker chair that would make her appear smaller and perhaps less threatening. Beaufort was obviously distressed. He hunched his shoulders and leaned forward in the Canadian rocker, apparently listening. "Did you notice or hear any signs of prowlers before this week? Do you think your dog kept things under control?"

Beaufort looked up at Woodman but the sheriff remained standing, facing the south windows. He didn't turn. Beaufort shrunk further into his jacket and looked at Amy. "I chose Margaret because she seemed large enough to keep people from breaking in. And she barked when anyone came near the house. But then she disappeared and there were those cars in the night and since then I know someone has been prowling around. I hear them. I see flashlights at night. I hear leaves rustling in the daytime. There were rustlings today. That's why I shot.''

Again he looked at the sheriff but Bent continued to look out the window. ''This afternoon I heard those rustling sounds. Like bears in the leaves.'' How often had city-bred Alex Beaufort ever heard a bear walking in the leaves? ''But I couldn't see anything. That's why I got out the gun and read the directions and loaded it. When I saw something moving, I shot. All I hit was the dog.''

Amy controlled her reaction. Only a dog. What kind of human being was this Alex Beaufort? But while he was talking they might get answers to some questions. So she asked, ''You heard these rustlings in back of your house? By the garage and driveway?''

''Yes. I looked out all the windows, even those in the upstairs rooms. I couldn't see anything. But the sounds didn't stop. Something was out there.''

''You said cars at night. On just one night or several nights? Was this before or after your dog disappeared?'' Amy kept her voice low and spoke slowly. Beaufort's body as well as his eyes made her think of a spooked horse, ready to bolt at any moment.

''Cars at night? I saw headlights up on the road, and the next time I saw more headlights. But Margaret didn't bark. And then they drove away.''

''Do you remember what night that was?'' Amy forced herself to keep speaking quietly.

''What night? Sunday night. Last Sunday night. I set the timer so I wouldn't forget to turn on the TV for *Masterpiece Theatre* but when I saw the headlights of a car parked up on the road, I didn't turn my lights on. I waited in the dark until the car drove away. It was headed out.''

Beaufort appeared more relaxed. Talking seemed to ease his tension.

Amy hoped Woodman wouldn't make any sudden moves or blurt out the questions they both wanted answered. ''Were your lights on when you saw the two cars?''

''Oh, no. That was the next night. I was sleeping but the headlights shone in on the white wall and awakened me. It was almost two a.m. I didn't turn on any lights. The trucks went out to the highway.''

Amy gripped the arms of the chair and struggled to keep her voice gentle. ''It was Monday night or early Tuesday morning when the lights awakened you?''

''Yes.''

''Alex, on Sunday night, when you had the timer set so you wouldn't miss *Masterpiece Theatre,* were you resting or asleep during the hour before nine p.m.?''

''I don't take naps. I never take naps. I was watching the tide come in. That's why I had no lights on.'' Beaufort's voice was almost shrill. That question disturbed him. Was it the word *nap,* not spoken but implied?

Amy said another silent prayer that the sheriff would be patient for a few more minutes. ''Was it a car or a pickup you saw Sunday night?''

''A car or a truck? All I saw were the headlights. Well, I did see the rear as it drove off. I guess it was a truck.''

''You reported your dog missing on Sunday. So Margaret wasn't here to bark when you saw those headlights Sunday night. Is that right?'' Amy watched Beaufort's hands clench and unclench.

''The whole idea was stupid. I never wanted to come

here. I never wanted a dog. I told them it wouldn't work.'' Beaufort leaned toward Amy, his voice shrill again, breathing in gasps. ''She should never have gotten married.'' He leaned back in the rocker as though he'd blown an obstruction out of his throat and his heart.

Bentley Woodman turned quietly but waited. Amy kept her voice soft and low. ''You've been uncomfortable here.''

''I hate this place. There are noises. I've never lived alone before. It wasn't right for my mother to get married again. She's too old for that kind of thing and it broke up our home and that man bought this place and I hate it here.''

Beaufort slumped deeper into his large, fleecy jacket and looked up at the sheriff. ''Are you going to arrest me for shooting at Mr. Adams?''

''Yes. That I must do. Do you have an attorney?''

EIGHTEEN

JEB PARKER WAS raking the driveway when Amy drove back to the harbor. He leaned the rake against the shed and said, "Come with me. Those two are so deep in old forks they won't know you're back." He led Amy around the building and up the steps to the ledges. "Sit a bit. No black flies here."

They sat in silence on one of the long plank benches, looking out at the islands beyond the channel, feeling cool salty breezes coming in from the sea and heat radiating from the stretch of sun-warmed rocks.

"Something's upset you," Jeb said.

Amy watched the gentle surf washing over the shore rocks below the roadway. On this May afternoon, low waves broke with steady, rhythmical washing sounds. Soothing. Here within the harbor the ocean waves could be high and wild and dangerous. Fishermen and their coastal neighbors never fully relaxed. They didn't feel threatened by the power of the tides and the winds and waves but they knew these as forces to respect.

"Upset? That's mild," Amy said. "I'm feeling tumbled, topsy-turvy, shaken. Since the moment I discovered that boy's body in the sawdust shed, I've been getting jolts and jabs and surprises from all sides. I have a Rip Van Winkle feeling as though I've awakened suddenly to discover multitudes of things that have been going on while I've been dozing. I haven't had time to absorb what's going on, to sift and sort and make sense out of what is happening and what has happened.''

Amy turned toward Jeb, spread out both hands and shrugged her shoulders. "For example...listen to this. Bent Woodman wanted me with him when he went out to Allen's Point to question Alex Beaufort. Felt a woman's presence might calm the man and make it easier to question him. That man is an emotional basket case. He's what my father used to call a 'weak Willie' or a 'namby-pamby.' Does anyone use those phrases anymore? When we finally got the man calmed down enough to talk, he told us he was distressed because his mother recently remarried and pushed him out.

"Jeb, this man must be almost fifty years old. Apparently he was mothered and smothered and taken care of until he became, or at least felt, helpless. Then mama, who must be seventy, decided to get married. She didn't want a 'child' around the house, didn't want to play mummie anymore. So she and her new husband tossed around a lot of money and stuck Beaufort, a city man who has never been independent, in an isolated cottage on the coast of Maine where even the morning breezes in the trees sound to him like invaders. He came here because he's used to doing what he's told to do, but this man is scared to death.''

Jeb tilted his cap to the back of his head, smiled at Amy and asked, "Why does this bother you so much?"

Amy started to say she wasn't bothered and then, after a pause, she said, "Everything is bothering me. I can't seem to stay detached. And I don't much like myself this week. Yesterday I learned that Lou Fullerton, who is seventy, is living with Graham Ford, the artist who summers on Ward's Pond. I've never thought of Louella

Fullerton except as wife and then widow of Paul Fullerton.''

"I know. I knew the Fullerton boys," Jeb said. "Don't know as anyone ever heard a one of them laugh. Polite smiles now and then. Paul more than his three brothers. My Uncle Joe used to tell us that belly laughs were the key to sanity. Warned us to stay clear of folks who'd forgotten how to laugh. Or never learned.''

They sat in silence again. Amy watched a lobster boat half circle a sailboat, both heading in toward the wharf. Jeb placed his calloused hand over hers and asked, "What's really bothering you?"

"My safe, quiet, easy-to-deal-with world has been shaken by too many mixed-up, troubling happenings. Too much all at once." Amy turned toward Jeb. Her hand rose to her throat and her fingers drummed on her collarbone. "I'm sixty years old. Since Wednesday morning when I got caught in this turmoil, I keep feeling that I've lived in a cocoon for fifteen years or more. A cocoon with arrested development. I don't know what has been or is going on in Granton. I've lost contact with people because I stopped making contacts. Lou Fullerton was a friend. She was good and kind to me when I was in love with Dort. The kind of friend I needed. But after I came back to live in Granton, I made no effort to rekindle our friendship. Yesterday, when we were up at that farm, I wasn't able to tell the sheriff whether Lou was alive or dead. I'm ashamed.''

"Go on," Jeb said.

"Go on? Go on where? What I'm trying to tell you is that I don't know where I am. I can't get that dead boy out of my mind. I keep seeing him dumped in that shed like a bag of grain." Amy stood up and stepped over to a bed of daffodils backed by the dark ledge. She knelt beside them and began to break off the faded blossoms. When she looked up at Jeb, he tilted his head back and waited for her to continue.

"I keep seeing that dog straining against a chain up there in Fullerton's barn, left with no food or water. And today I find out that Arthur and Stanley Waldron have been watching my driveway at night."

"Amy, the last time I saw you off balance was when you came down here right after Monty left. Are you telling me you've been acting, that you've been shut down, just coasting for years? Is it the murder or is it spending hours with Dort Adams this week that you've found you're not ready to cope with?"

Jeb extended a hand and Amy stood up beside him. "You just said you're sixty years old but you made it sound like ninety. Why are you trying to maintain an image of Amy as the cool, competent Creighton? Can't you just *be*? Hellfire and damnation, woman. You used to be so alive you wore out everyone around you. You think somebody put you in that cocoon? Not so. You wove it. And you can crawl out. If you want to."

Jeb Parker was a quiet man. A man of few words. Amy stared at him and then at the faded flowers in her hand. Down below, Carrie and Tim looked up and waited. They'd come around in time to hear Jeb's "hellfire and damnation...."

Carrie waved and caught their attention. Jeb and Amy started down the steps to the back lawn. In answer to Carrie's "You helped the sheriff?" Amy told them briefly of the shotgun episode and the reasons Beaufort had given for his distress and irrational behavior. Then she turned to Tim. "You look like a different man. What did you see and discover?"

"Mrs. Parker is going to loan me several special

pieces for the museum exhibit I'm preparing,'' Tim answered. "She has exactly what I want and never expected to find. Later we may do some cash dealings. Right now I'm elated. It's a long time since I've spent an afternoon with someone who shares my feelings about old china and silver.''

Amy looked at Carrie for confirmation of Tim's pleasure. Carried nodded and said, "Message from Dort. He won't get to your house until seven. Wanted me to tell you he talked with Lou Fullerton this afternoon and with the lawyer the Stillmans hired and sent up. Asked me about Parker Waldron—Arthur Waldron's father. I looked up his obituary in my Parker scrapbook. Parker drowned off Bean Island twenty years ago. There was talk of foul play because of bruises on his head but nothing ever came of it.''

Carrie noticed Jeb's frown and added, "I told Dort I'd talk with Jeb about it. Maybe between the two of us we can remember more. That branch of the Waldron family lived up in Rockland, but Parker was a fisherman. Dort will call back to see what else we remember.''

As she and Tim settled into the car for the drive back from the harbor, Amy saw the bag of cheese and cookies and, on impulse, suggested driving out to Allen's Point. They sat on the rocks below Beaufort's empty cottage. As they shared the food, Amy told Tim some of the theories she and Dort had discussed concerning the murder. William Stillman could have been killed here at the point. Lab tests showed the clay on the dog to be the same as that found on Stillman's clothes. Now the state police needed soil samples from here at the point and from pickup trucks.

"You can't go around peering into people's trucks and scraping out bits of dirt, can you?'' Tim asked.

"What are the state police doing, what's their role? Don't they handle the murders? Doesn't Maine have special homicide detectives or such?"

Amy nibbled at another cheese cube. "Good questions. I've focused mostly on 'why' issues. Why did Stillman come to Granton, Maine? You said he told you he was trying to locate family or ancestors and had papers with information. Which haven't been found. Why would someone kill a nice young college student who was looking for information about his family, maybe his birth parents?"

Tim took the last cookie. "Whose job or profession or status would be ruined if an unacknowledged child showed up? A school teacher? A minister? Politician? Can you think of an individual or local family focused on maintaining a reputation who might fear having their public image shattered? Enough to kill to keep a twenty- or twenty-one-year-old secret? Does that make sense?"

"Not to me," Amy answered. "But lots of things other people find sacred don't register with me. We have residents who believe they're God's chosen people, the righteous ones who never sin. Some may be irrationally afraid of sin or emotional excesses. Fear of discovery could include fear of failure or fear of loss. How about money? If someone paid the Stillmans to adopt a local child, could the Stillmans have used that for blackmail? None of these ideas sounds like Granton." Amy folded the napkins and plastic bags and replaced them in the carrying bag. "But murder doesn't sound like Granton, either."

Tim watched Amy folding the wrappings so they wouldn't blow away and litter the shore. Suddenly he said, "Wait. Don't move. I'll be right back." He climbed back over the rocks, turned, looked both ways, then ducked down to poke into a crevice.

Using a small branch, Tim pulled out a candy wrapper that had been stuffed between the rocks. He folded it inside his handkerchief and put it in his pocket. "Silly, maybe. But that's the kind of candy bar I gave Stillman. He said thanks and put it in the pocket of my jacket. I half-noticed the wrapper as we climbed down here. Probably a long shot but if Stillman's fingerprints are on it, it might show that he was here on these rocks."

On the ride back to Granton, they batted ideas back and forth, knowing many were utterly ridiculous, but hoping for at least one breakthrough to a lead that could be followed. As they approached the sawdust shed, Amy slowed down and turned into Ira Bellhouse's driveway. Amy and Tim both stepped out and looked across at the wide-open front of the mill building.

"Did you ever teach school?" Tim asked.

"No."

"I did. For two years. I loved it. Teaching felt right." Tim kept his gaze on the mill shed. "My students liked 'just suppose' games. We did these a lot on field trips. The kind of thing we were doing on the drive up here, but with the kids we moved and acted things out. That seemed to get more ideas bubbling up and out. It's the hand and brain theory of learning."

For a few minutes they stayed with their own thoughts and then Tim asked, "Do you know the people who live here? Would they have a wheelbarrow we could use?"

Amy said, "Ira's gone up-country but he won't mind if we borrow his wheelbarrow." She led the way around the house and down the slope to the tool shed beyond the outhouse. The wooden slide latch opened easily.

Amy noted that Ira, with his neat habits, had washed the shed window before he left.

Tim lifted the wheelbarrow down from its hanging rack on the wall and trundled it outside. He said, "Now just suppose we brought Stillman's body here in a car. Anyone driving past wouldn't see a car or truck down here below the house. Now we play just suppose. From down here behind the house we have to get him, and he's heavy, across the road and up into that shed. Let's go."

Amy was about to close and latch the tool shed door when the metal wheel clunked against the flat stone slab doorstep in front of the outhouse. "Stop, Tim. Wait. Stay right there."

On the morning she discovered the body, Amy noticed that the stone step by the outhouse was slightly out of line. A loaded wheelbarrow could have tunked that step enough to show a spot of raw earth. Were there any traces of leaves or grass or soil on that wheelbarrow? Caught in the hub of the wheel? Ira Bellhouse would never have gone up-country leaving dirt in or on any of his tools or equipment. And he probably would have noticed if that step had been out of kilter before he left.

Tim's "just suppose" might be the lead they'd hoped to find.

NINETEEN

TIM STEPPED BACK and waited, still holding the wheelbarrow handles. Amy knelt and reached out to feel around the hub of the wheel and exclaimed as her fingers touched shreds of dried grass and several small twigs.

"Someone has used this wheelbarrow since Ira left, used it recently. Let's lift it back into the shed, Tim, so we don't shake anything off." She moved around to lift the front end. "Look down here. See that clinging dirt? Ira Bellhouse is compulsively neat about his equipment and his tools." Amy pointed at the wrought iron hook on the outhouse. "Before he left, Ira oiled that latch. He washed the window in the tool shed. He would never have put this wheelbarrow up in that rack without wiping it clean with an oiled rag. If we hadn't played your game, no one would have noticed this. The summer renters certainly wouldn't."

Amy touched one bit of clay and sand sticking to the inside of the wheelbarrow. "The police lab crew needs to check this. Maybe it has no connection with the soil found on Stillman's clothes, but finding it here and knowing Ira's tidy habits is too much of a coincidence. Let's set this inside, carefully."

After she slid the tool shed latch in place, Amy showed Tim the sliver of brown soil showing at one edge of the stone step. "If we hadn't teased Ira for years about being nasty neat, I'd never have noticed that. It's only a slight deviation but when I saw it Wednesday morning after I found the body, I tried to think of a logical explanation. Then the sheriff interrupted, shifted my attention to other things. When you bumped the metal wheel on the doorstep, the sound brought back a picture of the edge of that stone. With something heavy in the wheelbarrow, such a bump could have jarred the step out of line."

"One strong man, one desperate or frightened man, could have moved Stillman's body with that wheelbarrow, but it would have been easier with two," Tim said. "But why use such a roundabout method? Why not drive right up to the sawdust shed instead of coming down into this back yard?"

Tim looked across the Bellhouse back lawn to the gravel driveway that ended at the foot of the slope. The garage, set at an angle, required a turn to drive a vehicle inside. Beyond the firm gravel driveway, a narrow, two-tire track continued on into the woods. This was the access road Ira used to haul out his winter wood, the track local hunters used during bird and deer seasons.

Tim and Amy looked at the slope of the driveway. The lower end was not visible to cars or trucks passing on Harbor Road.

"What did the pathologist estimate as the time of death?" Tim asked.

Amy stared at him. "I don't know. I didn't hear anyone say. Perhaps I wasn't listening. My head kept asking, 'Why?' Not much else registered. The boy was dead before his body was placed in the sawdust shed. He had eaten about four hours before he died. But if anyone mentioned the time of death, I didn't hear it. Why?"

"The body was placed in the shed Monday night but

his last meal could have been lunch, not dinner.'' Tim looked around the yard again. "Suppose the killer had to wait, needed to hide the body until it was dark?''

"We can ask Dort or the sheriff. They'll know the time of death. They've seen the autopsy report. And I'd better call, now, about the wheelbarrow. We'll go over to the mill office.''

But the office was closed. The car clock showed it was past six. The next phone was up the road at Norton's. When Amy drove in, the three Norton children were outside by the driveway so she asked them if she might use their phone. They exchanged glances and then the older boy asked if he could make the call for her. Could both parents be drunk at this hour? At suppertime?

Amy wrote out the sheriff's number. "Please tell the man who answers the phone to send someone down here to Morse Mill right away. I'll wait so you can tell me what he says.''

Tim stepped out of the car and asked if he might stroke the kitten held by the younger boy. "What's his name?''

"It's a she. Mom says we can't keep it because girl cats have kittens.'' The boy cuddled the furry creature under his chin. "We call her Morsey 'cause we found her at Morse Mill. In the sawdust shed.''

"All alone?'' asked Tim. "No mother cat? No other kittens?''

"We didn't see any others, did we, Josie? Morsey was crying. That's why Josie and Kent went in to find her. It's kind of spooky in there.''

Josie added, "They found a dead man in there the next day. Kent says he must have been there, under the sawdust, when we went in to find the kitten. That's scary.''

Amy rubbed a finger over the kitten's head and kept her eyes on the face of the boy holding her. ''Was it after school when you heard Morsey crying?''

''Later. About this time of day,'' Josie said. ''We went for a walk because mom wasn't feeling well. Sometimes we go down to Mr. Bellhouse's place. He lets us play with his cats and he tells us stories about the dogs he used to have. But he went away last week to his summer job.''

''Mr. Bellhouse used to have twelve beagles but he never had any children.'' The younger boy seemed to gain confidence from the purring kitten and joined in the conversation. ''He says children are treasures. Better than gold. I wish he hadn't gone away.''

''Someone else is going to live in his house this summer,'' Josie said. ''We don't know whether they'll let us visit or not. Maybe they think kids are a nuisance. We like to play with the cats. Mr. Bellhouse likes to have us come down to pat and play with them. He says cats are like children. They need loving or they don't eat well.''

The older boy, Kent, came out of the house and quietly closed the door. ''The man on the phone said the sheriff is in Granton and he'll get the message to him right away. Is it something about the murder? We were in that shed the day before they found the body.'' He paused and looked at Amy. ''Mrs. Creighton, you found him.''

''Yes, I did. Josie told us it was about this time of day when you found the kitten in that shed.'' Amy and Tim both watched the children's faces. ''Did you notice, as you went in to find the crying kitten, whether any of the pussy willow branches by the shed were twisted and broken?''

"Benjie did that," Josie said. "Well, he started it and then all of us went at the bushes. Benjie wanted a branch with the caterpillar things on it but they wouldn't break. They just bent. Kent and I helped him. We twisted and pulled and then Kent found a hunk of broken glass and we sliced some off. That was when we heard the kitten crying. I guess we made a mess."

"I'm sure Mr. Morse won't mind," Amy said. "We wanted to know how flexible willow bushes happened to get broken and bent at about the same time someone placed Bill Stillman's body in that shed. You've helped us. Did you notice anything else while you were there? Move anything? Pick up anything?"

The three children looked at each other and shook their heads. Kent said, "I don't think so. Josie and I went in. We had to wade through the sawdust to catch the kitten. I put it inside my jacket and then we both came back out."

Josie added, "We sat on the step and patted the kitten so she wouldn't be afraid of us and then we brought her home."

"She kept crying inside Kent's jacket but after we fed her she went to sleep." Benjie grinned up at them. "Then I named her Morsey. They let me be the namer."

Beyond the tangle of bushes and what had once been a hedge, Amy caught a glimpse of the sheriff's car. "Thanks for answering our questions. I think I'll find some special kitty food for Morsey because she helped, too."

Tim looked back, waved at the children. "You've added a few answers and raised more questions," he said to Amy. "What's the next 'why' on your mind?"

"Why that sawdust shed? With all the land and all the buildings on this peninsula, why was Stillman's body, his dead body, placed in the Morse Mill shed?" Amy turned into the Bellhouse driveway again and stopped behind the sheriff's car. "And the number one question. Why would someone in Granton, Maine, kill a twenty-year-old college student from Buffalo, New York?"

Sheriff Woodman and a deputy were leaning against the department car, talking across its roof. As Amy and Tim stepped out of her car, Dort Adams's pickup pulled up on the lawn beside them. Woodman looked tired and impatient, not pleased to see Amy.

"What is it you think you've found this time? More twigs on family trees? Bags and papers or just suppositions?"

TWENTY

WHEN SHERIFF WOODMAN heard the facts about the wheelbarrow and Tim's theory of how the body might have been moved, his irritation cooled. He didn't interrupt Amy's explanations of Ira's habits or Dort's confirmation of these. Bentley slipped back into the car and called for the lab crew. However, when Amy mentioned the shifted stone, the sheriff looked skeptical. Amy watched his expression change. Maybe the man was tired and hungry but she felt he wanted to brush aside the ideas she and Tim presented. Brush other people's ideas away as annoyances like the black flies that were buzzing around all of them.

"What did the autopsy tell you about the time of death?" Amy asked. "How long had the boy been dead before someone put his body in the sawdust shed?"

"Probably twelve hours," Dort said. "Stillman was lying on his side under the sawdust but he had been on his back for some hours following death."

"And you don't know where he was killed or where the body was between the time of death and the time it was dumped in that shed Monday night or Tuesday morning?" Amy directed her question to the sheriff but she also looked at Dort.

"That's what we're working on. That's why we're

here. Dort, let's have a look in the tool shed.'' Woodman moved toward the path around the back of the house.

Amy felt a flash of anger at being dismissed so abruptly but she caught Dort's wink. Bentley Woodman's behavior was officious, lacking in tact. Like a young bantam rooster taking charge of the whole hen yard. He had only been sheriff for nine months. Most of his deputies were taller and heavier than he was and Woodman was also aware that many local folks weren't sure a man brought up in Massachusetts should be the law officer of a Maine county. *Besides,* she said to herself, *I'm old enough to be his mother and boys do get fussed up. Let it go.*

She was smiling when she turned back to her car. Tim raised his eyebrows. ''Guess he put us in our places. So much for theories. Didn't his attitude irk you?''

''Yes. But I need my energy for other things.'' Amy looked at the bags still filling the back of her car. ''I've been driving around with that mulch in my car for days. Let's get going. It needs to be spread on my strawberries. The asparagus hasn't been weeded and already it's time to harvest enough for a meal. The sheriff is tired and he's probably being pressured. Dort will talk him loose.''

''Does Dort Adams ever get mad?'' Tim asked. ''He seems easy going and laid back but, as constable, he must find himself in nasty situations. He looks as though he could pick the sheriff up and shake him—and maybe would like to do just that.''

Amy made the turn off the main road before she answered. ''Dort has a temper but he also has a sense of humor. From the tales they tell around town, Dort Adams has stopped more violence with words, with his jokes, than with his muscles. He threw a man in the icy river one fall for abusing his horse. When he caught the banker's son shooting Lucy Feyler's cat with his BB gun, he carried the boy into his father's office and dumped him on the man's desk. But Dort listens to people, and, because he does, many times the anger and energy that might have caused trouble get blown out in words. Dort is liked and respected. Bentley Woodman acts like the cock-of-the-walk, but, from what I hear, he leans on Dort Adams's advice.

"Fidgets. What is that man doing in my yard?" Amy swung her car sideways to block her driveway. She stepped out and surveyed the yard. Joe Waldron's heavy pickup truck with its oversized tires was parked in front of her garage. Where was Chutney?

Tim stood by the car and watched Amy. She was angry but controlled. Then Chutney came racing up from the brook, tongue hanging out, too tired to bark. Amy hugged the dog against her thigh, stroking the dog's head and side, calming her with words.

Following Chutney, Ruth Waldron came up the path looking as out-of-breath as the dog. She wiped the black flies away with a vinegar-soaked towel and said, "I hope you don't mind. Your dog and I had a run out to the pond. It's wonderfully beautiful and peaceful out there. Except for these flies."

Before Amy could answer, Ruth noticed that Amy had blocked the driveway with her car. "You thought it was Joe, didn't you? Has he been here before?"

"Stanley and Arthur have been watching my house. I've no idea why but I don't like it," Amy said. "That's why seeing Joe's truck made me angry. He told us the other night that no one else drives this new vehicle. Let's go in out of these flies."

Introductions were made while Amy unlocked the

door. Tim went on to the office to call his father. In the kitchen, Amy waved Ruth to a chair at the long table and poured glasses of spring water from the refrigerator.

Ruth spoke quickly, without wasting time on meandering preliminaries. "The Waldron men are clannish. They stick together whether they're right or wrong. They may not like each other but, if one Waldron asks a favor of another, the answer is always yes. With Joe, the Waldrons always come first. That's the way it's been since I married him. I don't like it. It's aggravating, insulting. This week something is going on. Joe won't answer my questions. He went off this afternoon with Stanley. Said he won't be back until late tonight. That's why I have the Joe-only, damned expensive, unneeded, show-off, gas-guzzling truck.

"I couldn't locate Dort so I came to find you, to ask you to pass my information on to him." Ruth was hurrying but she had organized her thoughts. "The newspaper and radio reports said Stillman's body had been put in the sawdust shed on Monday night. Joe got a phone call just after supper on Monday. Told me he had to go out. Family business. He didn't come home until four a.m. Told me to shut up when I asked where he had been. Then he washed his new truck, inside and out, and he scrubbed his boots. That was Tuesday. On Wednesday, at suppertime, the boys and I had to be quiet so he could hear the news. In those broadcasts, the state police and the sheriff asked for information on persons, trucks, any unusual movements seen Monday night or early Tuesday morning.

"When I asked Joe if he had seen anything while he was out Monday night, if he had driven past the Morse Mill, he told me he had been at Stanley's house playing cards." Ruth paused, looked out the window, and took a deep breath. "I don't want to think Joe is a bad person. He's selfish and arrogant and his manners need improving but I can't believe he's evil. I live with him. I think he's afraid of being considered unmanly or some such rot by any or all of those Waldron cousins that infest this place. I think his loud mouth is for their benefit. I thought if Dort could talk to him...."

Ruth took a drink of water and placed the glass carefully in front of her. "I want to know where Joe and Stanley are today and what they're doing, what's going on. I'm tired of being treated like an unworthy, not-too-bright servant instead of a wife and partner." She drank the rest of the water and carried the glass to the sink. "Call it the turning of the worm. Joe said he was going to get a second job to pay for that truck, the truck he does not need. He hasn't done it. I'm putting part of my earnings away for the boys' education and I will not make a truck payment for him. Not even if it really is 'just this once.' Thanks for listening, Amy. You will tell Dort?"

"I will. He's coming for supper if the sheriff lets him free. They were down by Morse Mill when Tim and I came up from the harbor." As she spoke Amy thought how years of practice in protecting her space and privacy had developed her competency with words. Amy Creighton had become skillful at not lying by telling only part of the truth.

Amy moved her car so Ruth could turn and drive out and so Tim could do the same. He came out to the driveway once again wearing that tense, drawn look on his face. "My father wants to fly up to Maine tomorrow and ride back with me. What'll we talk about for twelve hours?"

"Start by talking to him as you talk to me. I enjoyed

your company this afternoon. So did Carrie Parker. Let your father enjoy your company. Tell him you like him. Tell him your feelings about teaching. Does he know how you scrounged about New York for years learning about china and old silver?'' Amy was tired. Her weariness made her impatient. She needed to stretch or swim or something. She was hungry and it was time to get the chowder on the stove.

''Did you ever ask your father how he acquired his expertise with words? How he developed a sixth sense about what books the public will buy? Get Sam Mozeson talking about books and time will fly. Try it.''

As Tim moved toward his car, Amy said, ''That candy wrapper. Did you give it to the sheriff?''

Tim took the handkerchief-protected candy bar paper from his pocket and passed it to Amy, thanked her for an afternoon of new experiences, and headed back to Westport Island.

When Dort Adams, followed by Chutney, came in shortly before eight p.m., he found Amy asleep on the living room sofa. Promising smells of fish chowder with bacon and onions came from the kitchen. The dog lapped Amy's face and she opened her eyes to find Dort towering above her. He said, ''Have you eaten? I can leave if you're worn out.''

Amy closed her eyes. ''I'm tired but I'm also hungry. Move over, Chutney.'' Dort took Amy's hands and lifted her to her feet. The dog dove between them and she fell against Dort. And stayed there. Dort rubbed the back of her neck and waited. ''Thanks, Dort. I'm still half-asleep.''

They crossed the hall to the kitchen and, without feeling a need to talk, Amy fed Chutney while Dort ladled chowder into the orange bowls. Amy flipped the switch on the coffee maker and filled the water glasses. They smiled at each other across the table and began to eat. Amy wondered if Dort was remembering, as she was, the years when the two of them had silently put meals together in this kitchen and eaten together at this table after hours of hiking and exploring and arguing.

When Dort rose to refill his bowl, he pointed to the counter by the stove where a candy wrapper was sticking out of a man's handkerchief. Amy explained, "Tim found it poked into a crevice in the rocks in front of Beaufort's place. Said it was the kind of candy bar he had given Stillman. Tim thought you might want to test it for fingerprints so he carried it in his handkerchief. It might show that Stillman was at Allen's Point."

Dort reached for Amy's bowl and when he set it, filled, in front of her, he asked, "Were you put out by Bent's shortness after you and Tim told him your ideas?"

"Briefly. Then I figured he was probably hungry. Who's on his tail?"

"The attorney the Stillmans sent up here is making noises and is talking to reporters. He sounds like old beans and cow plops to me but you should see the car he's driving!" Dort buttered another pilot cracker. "I think Bent's tired of hearing that a man from Massachusetts doesn't understand how to handle crimes in Maine. Augusta is after him because he hasn't come up with whoever is responsible for the vandalism on the peninsula and the moneyed cottage owners keep after Augusta. Give Bent a few more years and we'll have a damned good sheriff. But he does get puffy and pompous."

"You asked Carrie about Parker Waldron. Oh, fidgits. I forgot what I needed to tell you. Ruth Waldron was here. She wanted to talk to you but couldn't reach you this afternoon so she asked me to pass along her information. She thinks Joe and his Waldron cousins know more about what was going on Monday night than they have told anyone thus far.''

Amy related her conversation with Ruth. And while Dort was sorting those facts in his mind, she remembered Carrie saying that Parker Waldron's death had been questioned but no charges had been filed. Parker was Arthur's father. Who was Joe's father? Was Stanley a first cousin or a second?

''Ruth Waldron should have a husband like Doc Kelling,'' Dort said. ''Joe is a 'me-first.' Always has been and I don't think he'll change colors at this stage. Remember, we saw Joe's new truck yesterday when we came through Hurley's Hollow, parked at Mel Driscoll's trailer? I talked with Mel this morning. He had been drinking. Thinks he 'loaned' Joe cash to make a truck payment. Mel's money is gone but he has no receipt. All he can remember is that Joe brought him home, offered him a drink, and said he needed cash, just this once. Mel has only his pension, hardly enough money to keep his own truck running. Well, it might be enough if he'd stop drinking.''

''Did the sheriff or the state police find any information on the adoption?'' Amy asked. ''Do county records have a copy of the birth certificate for the baby the Stillmans adopted?''

''The Stillmans' lawyer has a birth certificate for a baby boy, born in Augusta, Maine, mother Olga Kouvalata, father P. Waldron,'' Dort said. ''The only P. Waldron we found was Parker. He died at age forty-four, almost twenty years ago. If Parker had been the father of a baby put out for adoption, what possible reason would there be to kill that child? Now?"

Amy poured coffee and moved her cookie jar nearer to Dort. "Ever hear of a P. A. Waldron? I remember seeing that name in the courthouse when I was checking my deeds and property lines the year I sold land to finance building my office. Someone listed as P. A. Waldron owned land here in this county, had either just bought or sold land that year. Thirteen years ago. Wasn't there a plumber or electrician named Philip Waldron in Waldoboro? This coastal area is full of Waldrons. But what would be a motive for murder? For killing a young man with all his life ahead of him?"

Dort looked tired. Tired and sad. He held his coffee mug up against his chin with both hands, breathing in warmth and aroma. "My son is twenty-six. The night we all took a look at Stillman's body to see if anyone recognized him, I was filled with anger that any person could destroy someone so young and healthy. Could take away his life and his future. I felt glad that my son Abel turned out well after all the bumps he suffered."

Dort put his mug down and leaned toward Amy. "Stillman had his bumps and they sound bad. I talked with a counselor at his college and one at his boarding school, prep school. His parents bought him things and ignored him. They sent him to camps in the summer. Left him alone when he was home. No friends. No relatives. The Stillmans gave him room and board and things but, other than that, they had a 'don't bother us' attitude. Living that way must have been a kind of murder."

"What kinds of papers do you think the boy was carrying in that canvas bag?" Amy asked. "Bag....Beaufort said Stanley Waldron was looking for a bag. Is it too crazy to wonder if Stanley Waldron was looking for Stillman's missing bag? Oh, fidgits. I'm probably thinking this because I don't like the man. I find him unpleasant. The man avoids eye contact.''

TWENTY-ONE

DORT PUT TWO COOKIES side by side on his plate and regarded them thoughtfully. Amy waited and watched him pick up the cookie on his left and begin to bite around its edges. Long ago on their picnics, he told her nibbling makes cookies last longer.

"Bent asked why you're so interested in this investigation." Dort sat back and watched for Amy's reactions. "He asked why you didn't go back to work and stop asking questions."

"And you told him...."

"Well, I didn't tell him you've been asking questions since you started talking. I did tell him you didn't like unanswered questions. Never had. Told him about the time you kept digging into old land records until you found who held title to that bog hole next to the high school when the superintendent planned to drain and fill it and put an end to the science teacher's amphibian project.

"Used that to show Bent you weren't an interfering busy body. Wanted him to see that he and the state police could benefit from the fact that you look at things from different angles, tackle problems Amy Creighton's way."

"And Bentley Woodman didn't buy it."

"Maybe he was tired and hungry?"

"Maybe he was just being Bentley Woodman," Amy said. "I've heard town talk, heard about your disagreements with the sheriff. I haven't interfered in anything that's been going on since I found the boy's body Wednesday morning. Each time I've called the sheriff's office, I've had good reason for doing so. Does the man feel threatened by questions? By a woman asking questions about something he hadn't thought of? That's Woodman's problem. It's not helping us put pieces together. Do you know anything, have any information on how Stillman got from Wiscasset to Granton? About what happened after Tim dropped him off down there on Route One?"

"Yes. A couple of men headed for Belfast picked him up and let him out at the Granton turn-off," Dort said. "They called in after the radio and TV request for information."

"Did they notice the bag the boy was carrying?"

"We asked about that. According to both men, when they let Stillman out on Route One Sunday night, he was carrying a knapsack," Dort said. "No one has called with information about giving him a ride down the peninsula. We're still asking."

"Dort, my mind is skittering again. I haven't asked about Margaret. No. I won't use that name. How is the dog?"

"She's OK. Hurting. Doc dug birdshot pellets from her haunches so I left her there. I like that dog. And you were right about her leaping into the back of a pickup as though she'd been taught that's where dogs ride. I had to coax her to ride up front with me when I picked her up at Doc Kelling's today."

Amy refilled their coffee cups. Dort set two more cookies on his plate and said, "Let's go back to Stanley

Waldron. He owns a house on Allen's Point Road. He
also owns the ocean view lot next to Beaufort's place,
but that piece of salt water frontage is too narrow to meet
the new ordinances for a septic tank drainage field and
the required set-backs for buildings. Beaufort says Stanley has been trying to talk him into buying that land,
telling him it would increase the value of the cottage. I
think Beaufort's afraid of Waldron. He never did want
to live away from the city and he told us he doesn't
want to stay on that lonely point anymore.''

"Doc Kelling said Beaufort might do better out there
if he had a blond housekeeper instead of a dog.''

"Do you remember exactly what Beaufort said about
Stanley's coming on his property looking for a bag?''
Dort asked. "What kind of bag? Bag of what? And why
on Beaufort's land?''

Amy took the soup bowls to the sink and rinsed them.
She dried her hands as she came back to the table and
then folded and refolded the towel. "Beaufort was
fussed up about hearing what he called rustling sounds,''
she said. "Couldn't see anything or anyone but said he
kept hearing noises. After you left to take the dog to
Doc Kelling's and before Woodman and I drove in,
Stanley Waldron was there. Told Beaufort he was looking for a bag he'd lost the week before. Wait a minute.
I think Beaufort said, or implied, that Waldron had come
to the cottage before today looking for that lost bag. But
he couldn't tell us what kind of a bag it was.''

"From what he told Woodman on the way to county
jail, Beaufort hadn't wondered or asked why Waldron
had lost something on his cottage property,'' said Dort.

They sat in silence, processing this thought. Amy pictured Beaufort going from window to window trying to
see what might be behind or beside his cottage.

"If Stillman was killed down there at the point, it seems to me the killer would have taken the bag," Amy said. "But if the boy slipped and fell on the rocks, it could have startled and shocked whoever was with him so he or they didn't think of the bag until later. Could the tide have taken it?"

"Maybe Stillman hid it, put the bag and the papers he needed in a safe place before he...before he met someone? The boy could have made a phone call to someone in Granton. Could have called before he came to Maine. Where was William Stillman Sunday night and Monday morning, between the time he left Route One and the time someone dumped his body in that shed?" Dort's frown shifted to a wry smile. "In a town where seven people notice if I talk to a woman for ten minutes and ask me if I have a date when I buy two steaks, why hasn't anyone mentioned seeing a stranger?"

"Some people notice more than others. One observant woman reminded me this week that I'm still wearing a wool plaid shirt I bought in Hank Merchant's store and he went out of business twelve years ago. Have you or Woodman asked Hattie Howard if she noticed anything different or unusual about the cars and trucks that passed her place Sunday night or Monday morning? Familiar cars with more passengers than usual?"

Dort looked at his watch and at Amy's clock. "Too late to do that tonight. And you look done in. Could you be free to ride over with me in the morning?"

They cleared the table. Amy put away the chowder and the pilot crackers. Dort took the coffee mugs to the sink and then came back to the table for another cookie. This was the kind of after-meal routine the two of them had carried out hundreds of times in this room during their high school and college years. They moved back and forth in the long kitchen with the ease of good dancers.

Before Dort went through to the hall, he turned to Amy with an expressionless face and asked, ''Think you and I might be able to spend a whole day together without arguing? Think maybe both of us have mellowed?'' He left without waiting for an answer.

TWENTY-TWO

CLEANING UP didn't take long. Amy turned out the kitchen light, stepped outside, and pinned the dishcloth and towel to the porch line. Chutney rubbed against her. The bright stars appeared smaller on clear nights when millions of them twinkle-peppered the sky. Someday she'd take time to learn the patterns in the heavens, learn why the view of the sky from her back steps changed each month. Someday she'd begin to step outside at the same hour each night and observe the sky above her part of the Sacaja valley.

Something splashed in the brook. Chutney stiffened but stayed at her side. Amy felt the silence as a soft, comforting cloak, a welcome, peaceful cushion between her and the world. In this quiet yard, as a child and as an adult, Amy had soaked up tranquility, sitting alone in the darkness.

Poor Beaufort. For him, space and isolation and woodland noises fostered fear. How many of the sounds he heard were natural—wind in the trees, surf against the rocks—but were magnified by his mind? If he dreaded being alone at night in that cottage, why had he kept that affectionate, well-behaved dog outside? Why did Beaufort appear to be afraid of Stanley Waldron? He seemed to trust Bentley Woodman in his brown uniform. An authority figure?

It was still Friday. Broken sleep last night and too many happenings throughout the day made Amy feel it must be Saturday or Sunday. After her eyes adjusted to the darkness, she walked down around the house to her exercise bar. Chutney settled herself on the porch floor with a sigh. Amy had counted to eighty-two when Chutney growled, raced off to the front of the house, and began barking. Sharp, angry barking. Amy moved down and ran up the driveway. Chut was pursuing something or someone toward the road. A door slammed, headlights were turned on, and a vehicle with a strong-sounding motor headed out from her lane.

Amy called, "Stay!" to the dog as she ran around the curving driveway and out onto Hilton Road. Chutney whined but stopped and waited for her. Down the road, taillights of a pickup truck headed east. The light on the left was lighter. Broken plastic cover?

Back inside her house, Amy turned on the wall light beside the phone, flipped through the directory, and dialed Arthur Waldron's number. She told the woman who answered that she wanted to speak to Arthur.

"He's not back yet but I expect him soon. Would you like him to call you?"

Amy hung up with no explanation, no courteous comments. Hung up and quickly dialed Stanley's number. No answer. She tried Joe and Ruth's number. Ruth answered.

"This is Amy Creighton. Is Joe home now? Have you seen Arthur or Stanley in the last hour?"

"Are you all right? Is something wrong?"

"Right now, I'm hopping mad," Amy said. "Someone has been here, sneaking around my house. My lights were out. Chutney didn't catch him or them. A pickup truck headed toward East Granton. I'm OK, but answer my questions."

"Yes, to the first one. No, to the second." Ruth sounded as though she didn't want Joe to hear or understand.

"Were those Waldron cousins at your house earlier tonight?"

"The boys and I were up at the high school this evening. Went up with the Cargills," Ruth said. "Joe couldn't make it. He was out doing a job with his truck."

That was pretty good double-talk. "Thanks, Ruth. That may help. I'm going to find out why someone is watching my house."

Amy put the phone back on the cradle. Should she call Dort or the sheriff's office? Report sneaking prowlers? What could they do? The truck was gone. It could have turned off onto several other roads. Calm down and be glad Chutney has good ears and can sound savage. Lock up and go to bed.

It took time to relax and settle into sleep. Pictures floated across the screen of her closed eyelids. That name in the book of deeds—the P. A. Waldron who bought or sold land thirteen years ago. That could be checked. But not on Saturday, except by the sheriff. Tax records and voter records would have all the P. Waldrons listed. Land transfer records would tell when Stanley bought that Allen's Point house and the waterfront land next to Beaufort's cottage and when that went on the list of taxpayers. But the town office was also closed on Saturday.

What did she know about Arthur Waldron besides the fact that he wore proper business dress every day, even on Saturdays? That he insured most of the property on the peninsula, of summer people and year-round residents? In town and at the county seat she often saw Arthur's wife, sometimes called Emma the Great because of her size. But she couldn't recall ever talking with her. In Granton "they" said Arthur Waldron married for money, his father-in-law's money. They said Arthur and Emma used that Ramsdorff money to buy the old Gregg house in East Granton, the oldest Colonial house on the peninsula, and to restore and furnish the place. Garden clubs and history tours scheduled visits during the summer. Arthur's accounting and insurance office was also over in East Granton. He had built up a good business since his marriage, insuring houses, boats, and other vehicles of wealthy city folks along the river and along Sacaja Harbor.

Who had mentioned taxes today? Carrie Parker. She remembered that Stillman did taxes and accounting twenty years ago when he lived at the harbor. Had that Stillman, the one who adopted the murdered boy, known Arthur Waldron when he lived on the peninsula?

Saturday morning, the phone rang at six as Amy was headed for the garden to spread sawdust. Dort told her quickly, in short, terse sentences, that Stanley Waldron's body had been found. In his truck. At Ira Bellhouse's place.

TWENTY-THREE

STANLEY WALDRON DEAD? Last night Amy had been filled with anger at the man, believing he was the one sneaking around her house in the dark, driving off in a hurry when Chutney gave chase. Now Dort's crisp, quick message told her Stanley was dead, that his body had been found at Ira Bellhouse's place. Just three days after she had found Stillman's body in the sawdust shed across the road from Ira's house.

Amy locked up and drove out. She followed the familiar roads without needing to concentrate and allowed thoughts and questions to bounce back and forth in her head. People in and around Granton didn't like Stanley. His snarly manner and his habit of avoiding eye contact, never looking anyone in the face, were not conducive to building trust or friendships. Granton folks had not forgotten his butchering the Fullerton cattle, their prize steers. And his years behind bars. Had Stanley ever spent time with anyone who wasn't a Waldron? Still, who hated the man enough to kill him?

Wait. Dort said Stanley was dead. Dead, not murdered. Why was she thinking he had been murdered? Amy didn't like some of the thoughts she found bouncing around in her mind this week. Yesterday she had asked herself, "Why did William Stillman die while this nasty, unpleasant Stanley Waldron keeps on living?"

But feeling ashamed of such a thought hadn't kept it from popping back into her head again this morning. Before Dort's call. Now that surly man was dead. Were there links between the Waldrons and the Stillmans? Twenty years ago and now? Links that neither she and Dort nor the sheriff and the state police had been able to find?

Amy parked in the mill yard. Across the road in Ira's driveway, the sheriff's crew, two state police officers, the medical examiner, and photographer stood along the driver's side of Stanley Waldron's truck. Amy walked down the verge of the road until she was in front of the sawdust shed, then moved back and forth along the grassy shoulder until she was able to look across the road, look between the law officers, and get a clear view of the truck's taillights. The one on the left was broken. A triangular piece of red plastic was missing.

"That's Stan Waldron's truck. What happened? No sign of an accident." Amy turned to find Bert Norton and his son Kent beside her.

"Bert, are you sick?" Amy spoke without thinking but as soon as she sensed Bert's recoil, she added, "You don't look well at all. Stanley Waldron's dead. That's all I know. But you're right. There are no signs of an accident." Amy bent forward and spoke to Kent. "How's Morsey this morning?"

"Fine." Kent pointed to the sawdust shed. "Josie took Benjie in to check. He thinks there are more kittens, hungry kittens, in there."

Amy put her hand on Bert Norton's arm. "Your children are wonderful, Bert. Smart, polite, thoughtful. You and Doris have done a good job."

Bert looked surprised but his bloodshot eyes brightened. He turned toward the mill shed. "This neighborhood seems to be the center of attention this week. My father was a sheriff's deputy when they found Stan Waldron holed up in that shed after he killed the Fullerton's steers. Hid in there for a week. Waldrons brought him food. Then some kids saw the sawdust move and ran to tell old man Morse. Dad still talks about how the deputies lined up and tromped through the sawdust to force Stan out.''

"How many Waldron families are there?"

"Too many," Bert said. "Dr. Hank says they're not breeding as fast these days. He remembers old Will Waldron and his mean kids.''

The ambulance arrived with its red lights flashing and backed in behind Stan's truck. Bert asked Kent to go over and keep Josie and Benjie by the sawdust shed until the ambulance left.

Amy walked back to her car. Where was Dort? No sign of him or his truck. Stanley Waldron had a wife. Used to have a wife. Perhaps Dort had gone to break the news to her. Were Waldron wives kept in the background or did Waldron men marry cowed females? Ruth spoke about the turning of the worm—keeping her job and saving for the boys' education. Arthur and Emma had no children. Did Stanley?

She decided to swing into the village and pick up milk and dog food before going home. The early shoppers were discussing the news of Stan's death—with more imagination than actual facts. A man who had driven up from the harbor refuted a tale about a horrible head-on crash with an oak tree. Said Stan's truck didn't seem to have any new dents and it was neatly parked in Ira's driveway. His remarks encouraged a fresh round of speculations.

Al Curtis was packing groceries into a carton. "Some-one sick?" Amy asked.

"No. Hattie Howard's order. I'll take it around after the first run of shoppers leaves."

"Let me take them," Amy said. "I was planning to stop and see Hattie today. May as well do it now. I'll gather what I need." She moved toward the pet food shelves and then turned back. "You'll have to put the box on the front seat. The back is still full of bags of sawdust. Haven't found time to spread it yet."

The Howard farm was on the east end of what was now called the Old Road. Long ago, that town road had been named for the Olde family and their large farm along the river. But after all members of that family died or moved away and no one with the name Olde was left in Granton, careless copying and usage resulted in changed markings on newer maps. Land that had been cleared in 1820 for the Olde farm was now divided into small plots. Clusters of new homes were owned by commuting families. The school bus picked up more than a dozen children from that area each morning, the ones who waved to Hattie Howard when the bus stopped at the new sign before turning onto Harbor Road.

Amy carried the box of groceries to the side door that Hattie opened before Amy could knock. Hattie Howard moved slowly and balanced her frail body by touching walls, door frames, and backs of chairs. The two women exchanged greetings as Amy, who had done this many times before, put perishables in the refrigerator and dry goods in the big, old-fashioned pantry. Hattie uncovered a pan of sticky yeast buns. Amy poured coffee and carried the tray through to the sunny living room with the window overlooking the road. An extra cushion in Hattie's chair brought her high enough for a good view of passing vehicles.

"Your nephew Dennis claims you can tell the make and owner of every car that passes. Is that right?" Amy asked.

Hattie allowed as how she used to be able to do this. "But the young couples in those houses on the Olde farm change cars so often I get mixed up. They buy second-hand cars and trade up again before the year's out. Granton folks take care of their cars, fix them up and make do. I know those. Dort Adams has had that brown Dodge truck for seven years and Dr. Hank bought his green Chrysler ten years ago. Marvin Morse's still driving the Buick he bought for his second wife. My nephew's truck's got one red fender. Not hard to recognize."

"The sheriff's hoping someone would recall cars or trucks seen the night that boy from Buffalo was killed," Amy said. "He's hoping someone will remember noticing cars out late Monday night or cars seen on roads they don't usually travel."

Looking out the window, Amy watched a station wagon slow before the stop sign. The driver waved to Hattie. "Arthur Waldron's wife," Hattie said. "Emma picks up Stella Donne to help her keep that big house clean. Ever been inside the old Gregg house?"

"Once, as a child, with my grandmother. I remember it as big and chilly," Amy said. "I think Grandma Katherine was visiting one of the last living Gregg women. Later, when I came back to live in Granton, the house was empty. Did you visit there when you were a girl? See it in its good years?"

"Some would say the 'good years' started when Arthur and Emma bought it and began to restore it," Hattie said. "Parker Waldron told me once that from the time Arthur first saw that house, he said he was going to own it someday. He was just a boy then. You know Parker was named for his mother, Jennie Parker, one of Carrie's cousins. Nice man. He named his son for his wife Pauline Stearns, one of the Waldoboro Stearns. But I don't think he's ever been called anything but Arthur."

Hattie finished her coffee and placed the cup back on the tray. "Carrie and I talk about the old families. And the old houses. The Gregg house was in sorry shape for years. Those last two sisters had hardly enough for food and fuel. But that house was built by ship carpenters. Built from timber cut right there on that land. I've thought sometimes of asking Emma if I could have one more look inside the house. Probably never will. I'd like to see the hemlock windbreak they set in. The landscape man dug the young trees from my land. They must be good size now."

Amy's mind was still on Monday night. "Joe Waldron has a new truck—"

Hattie interrupted. "Expensive gas guzzler with those great big tires. Why would a man with a family to support go into debt for such a truck? What's the man use it for? Goes through this way when he's going to the harbor. Goes too fast and doesn't always stop at that sign. Last night he went speeding through after ten-thirty. I didn't see him come back. Could have gone home through the village."

"Did you notice Joe's big truck going through Monday night?"

"Monday night? Eva Parsons was here Monday," Hattie said. "We sorted out tatting she wants for the church fair. Yes, I saw Joe's truck go by, shortly after supper. I think he was alone. Couldn't be sure because he went right through the stop sign. Turned down toward the harbor. Stanley Waldron's truck was behind Joe's and Arthur followed in his wife's station wagon. He stopped at the sign and he waved. Arthur always had good manners.''

Hattie's hand went up in a high wave. ''It's Dort Adams and I believe he's coming in. Amy, will you get the door?''

TWENTY-FOUR

WHILE AMY WAS IN the kitchen getting Dort a cup of coffee and a warm, sticky, cinnamon roll, Hattie repeated her story about the parade of Waldron vehicles passing her house on Monday night.

"And why didn't you tell us this before?" Dort asked. "You listen to the local news. We've been asking about cars seen Monday night and you wait until Saturday to mention it." But Dort wasn't able to keep up his stern façade. Amy put a cup of coffee in front of him.

"I listen to the radio and what I heard the police ask for were reports of anything unusual," Hattie said. "Those Waldrons go up and down this road all the time. Well, I don't usually see three of them driving by at the same hour, three vehicles following each other, but what was there to report?"

"Did Amy tell you Stanley Waldron died last night?"

"Stanley died? My Ben always said Stan Waldron was too mean to die. Had a curdled heart. What'd he die of?"

"At the moment, it looks like someone struck him on the back of his neck, one solid blow that broke his neck. But that's not official. The sheriff and state police are working to find out more." Dort put his coffee cup down and looked at Hattie. "Did you see Stan Waldron's truck on this road last night?"

"I saw Joe's truck, that fancy thing he just bought. Went by after ten-thirty. Turned toward the harbor. No, I didn't see Stan's truck," said Hattie. "But I was in the kitchen some, making rolls. Do my cooking at night so's not to miss watching the world in daylight. See that shadbush over by the pines? I've watched every blossom unfold."

Hattie turned back from the window. "Stan was always a mean one, even as a boy. His father, Phineas Waldron, swore he'd beat the boy into righteousness. The Waldrons on this peninsula have always been great for going off on the heavy sinner path. Some in every generation." She smiled at Amy. "Remember the time you two spread those mallard eggs around? Ben named ours Adam. But old Will Waldron took on like you two had committed major sins against the Father, Son, and Holy Ghost—stealing from a wild duck's nest and invading his property to put an egg under his best settin' hen. Do you know, the week before that old man died he told Ben he knew God was going to get you and Dort for your sins." Hattie looked from Amy to Dort and back again. "Don't know what sins he had in mind besides stealing duck eggs."

Amy asked, "Does Stanley have a wife?"

"Yes. But I've never seen her. He was married when he came back after his spell in reform school." Hattie looked at Dort. "The story in town was that someone fixed it so Stanley went to that place instead of prison because that steer slaughter was his first offense. Anyhow, I've never seen his wife. Never heard her discussed. When Stan came back, he moved into the Amberley house down to the harbor on Allen's Point Road. I heard he bought it. Don't know when. Don't know if anyone else owned it after the Amberleys died. Maud Amberley was a Waldron, sister to Phineas.''

Dort asked, "Did Stanley have brothers or sisters? Any that are still living in this area?''

"None still around. The girls went to Michigan. Left school and left town. Stanley's twin, Steven, went up north. Millinocket or Milo. Don't think he's ever been back. Didn't come for his father's funeral. Poor old Priscilla. The only time she got out of that house was to go to church. Dr. Hank said she withered from neglect. Twins were ten when she died. Girls were older. They left soon after their mother died. I don't know whether Phin beat them like he did the boys. I do know who supplied the money so they could leave. Don't think Phin ever knew, ever found out who helped his unpaid housekeepers escape.''

Dort stood up. Hattie laughed as he dodged the hanging lamp. "You get bigger every year, Dort Adams. How come you don't get gray and wrinkled?''

"Country butter and lots of fish. You should try it, Hattie. Might be good for your knees. If you think of anyone or anything else you've seen, call me. Two deaths in one week have all of us on edge. Every bit of information is welcome.''

Amy carried the tray with coffee cups and plates to the kitchen and, as she rinsed these, Dort said, "Almost done? I'd like your opinion on a few thoughts.''

"Follow me home. I have milk in the car that needs to go in the refrigerator and I'm expecting two phone calls before noon.''

The answering machine by the kitchen phone was blinking and the office phone was beeping when Amy came in. She put the milk away and headed for the office. Message from Tim Mozeson. He had met his father at the airport and they were driving to Granton.

On the house phone, Polly Anderson was upset about another awful murder right here in our little town. Would Amy please call and tell her all about it? Carrie Parker's call was more urgent. She and Jeb had driven over to Stan Waldron's house when they heard about his death. Took a thermos of coffee. Rosabelle wouldn't open the door. They could hear her sobs and felt that a doctor or nurse might be needed. The third call, one Amy had been expecting, was from her long-time friend. June Kancapolos's plane had landed in Boston. She would head for Maine as soon as she checked with her home office. Cut the asparagus and warm up the pond.

Amy called Doc Kelling's office. Ruth Waldron answered. Amy repeated Carrie Parker's message. Was there a relative or friend who could or would go to Stanley's house, talk to his wife right away? Ruth said she and Joe would go down at once. If she could locate Joe. This Saturday he was supposed to be home with the boys. If not, she'd borrow Doc Kelling's car. Would Amy be at home if she needed help?

Amy relayed this information to Carrie Parker, who was glad to know someone was coming down to help that child. "Child?" asked Amy. "Do you know the woman? Hattie Howard said she'd never seen Stan's wife."

"Rosabelle was a child when Stanley brought her here. She's not more than thirty. A child to me," Carrie answered. "Jeb and I are really concerned. That poor girl has locked herself in and she is frightened. Keening like an Irish ghost."

TWENTY-FIVE

AMY HAD PUT AWAY her groceries and refilled the dog's water dish when she heard Chutney barking, joined by barking of another dog. From the kitchen window Amy saw Chut and Margaret—Maggie—race down the back lawn and into the brook. They stopped when the cold water hit their bellies, gulped and drank. Chut dashed at Maggie, who rolled over and under the water and then came up to the back lawn to shake. Chutney imitated the visitor and followed to stand beside her and shake in the sunshine. Maggie's thick, black coat required more dewatering than Chutney's sleek brown fur. Amy laughed aloud as the two wet dogs sat and looked at each other.

"I think they both like having company." Dort had come in from the front hall and stood behind her. His hand began to rub the back of her neck. How could a man of that size move so quietly? How could a gentle massage on the back of her neck stimulate stomach spasms and rubber knees—feelings she hadn't experienced for years?

Outside, Chutney took command. This was her territory.

"Chut's asking Maggie to come along to the pond. Watch." Amy's dog ran along the path, stopped, turned and barked and then headed on. Maggie cocked her head, gave a series of short barks, and followed. The dogs disappeared from view.

Amy turned but Dort didn't back away. He held out his arms and when Amy leaned against him, rubbing her nose in his soft, old flannel shirt, Dort wrapped his arms around her, gently, and moved his chin back and forth in her short, curly hair. This unexpected closeness felt comfortable, familiar, and exciting.

Without moving his arms or his body, Dort said, "I think Stan Waldron tied that dog in the barn and left her. The bed of his pickup is streaked with clay. He hauled soil for the nursery. We'll check with the Finleys about what he'd been working on and compare samples. I talked with Lou Fullerton this morning. Stan wrote threatening letters while he was doing time and, after he was released, she had nasty phone calls she believes he made. Stanley held onto his hate. No guilt. Hate festering for years. In his mind the Fullertons had him locked away. The Fullertons took his freedom."

Amy shuddered. "Just looking at Stanley Waldron always upset me. I felt liquid evil might seep out of his pores. For three days I've juggled information, facts, and theories in my head trying to prove to myself that Stanley Waldron killed the Stillman boy. But I couldn't come up with any motive beyond pure meanness."

Dort held Amy so lightly that standing in the circle of his arms felt right, felt protective but not restrictive. He said, "Lou Fullerton asked about you. Said her 'new' life was such a joy after all those dour years that she feels an evangelical urge to proclaim the rightness of taking risks, making changes. She joked about giving a Memorial Day address after the parade, inciting others to move on to fuller living. Maybe taking out a full-page ad in the newspaper or flying over the county dropping leaflets.''

"Tell her to exhibit that October painting. Have prints made. Show instead of tell. I thought I'd forgotten that part of living until I lifted the drape on that easel.'' She leaned back to look up at Dort. "How did you feel when you saw that scene?''

"I felt sixteen again, or twenty. With all the wildness, the heat and energy. No wonder Bent was confused and annoyed that day. He couldn't get straight answers from either of us. I never knew Lou Fullerton painted. But when I saw old Alfred in those cold mist paintings, I knew they had to have been done by someone who knew and felt the heartbreak and strain in that house, on that farm. I was sure then that Lou was the one who painted in that attic room.''

"Alfred? Alfred Fullerton?''

"Paul's oldest brother. The dourest of the dour. Even as a boy I saw the way Alfred looked at Lou. You remember, she was something to look at. Long legs. Wonderful smile. Through all those years she honored her marriage vows and, after Paul died, she did her year of mourning up on that hill. Then she went west for a winter in the sun. She told me that winter in the Arizona desert brought her back to life. Lou asked why you and I hadn't made similar discoveries.''

Chutney came racing up across the back lawn, headed for the driveway, barking madly. Maggie followed. Dort and Amy pulled apart and moved to the front hall. Tim Mozeson and his father were on the steps. A wave of pleasure and surprise caught Amy. Sam Mozeson looked exactly as she had pictured him during their years of telephone exchanges. She felt as though she had created this slim, gray-haired man with the severely trimmed goatee. And now he had appeared, in person, on her doorstep.

Amy spoke to Tim after introductions were made. "Go through to the kitchen with Dort. There's fruit juice in the refrigerator. I want Sam to see my office."

Sam Mozeson walked around the long, low-ceilinged room, looking at the equipment and arrangements, the glowing colors of the Persian rug and the wide, crescent-shaped desk. Then he sat in the green wing chair that faced the desk and asked, "Is this where you see me when we talk? I have a wine-red chair opposite my desk but, now that I've met you, I think you'd find it too large. I'm glad I came. I'll enjoy working with you even more now that I can visualize the room and you at that desk."

"I've enjoyed your son," Amy said. "Enjoyed hearing him talk about what he likes and likes to do. His face and his eyes light up when he speaks of teaching. I watched Tim's pleasure in handling old china and silver. He became a different person."

"On our drive up from Portland, Tim told me he enjoys teaching. Young children. Not college or prep school students. I had no idea. When he was teaching, I wore blinders. I didn't hear what he told me. I was waiting until he started doing something important. Something I considered important. Then I would pay attention. I told you I didn't know my son. How did I expect I'd learn who he was when I didn't tune in? Didn't listen. Just before we reached Granton, Tim asked how I learned to ferret out or sniff out books that would sell. Never knew he was interested. We'll have plenty to talk about on the drive back to New York."

"Can you remember to listen?" Amy asked. "Not sit and wait for a turn to talk? Can you listen to Tim with the concentration you give to discussions about your books or your business?'' She smiled so her questions didn't sound like criticism and then changed the subject. ''Let's join the others.''

Tim showed his father the blue-and-white cookie jar. Dort lifted the cover and offered Sam a cookie. When Amy slipped into her usual chair at the long table, she felt tired. As tired as though she'd done a day's work. And it wasn't eleven o'clock yet.

''My son has been filling me in on your activities this week connected to the murder investigation.'' Sam looked at Dort as he spoke. ''And he's been pointing out rivers and ponds along the way. I can see why Amy prefers working here.'' Sam waved at the view from the row of windows, the green lawn above the flowing water. The two dogs, back from the pond, stood in the brook, gulping water and cooling their bellies. ''Your dogs?'' Sam asked Amy.

''Chutney, the brown one, is mine,'' Amy said. ''Maggie, the black one, is temporarily unclaimed. She has been at the vet's, recovering from abuse and Dort....'' Amy turned. ''Dort, you stopped at Doc Kelling's and picked up Maggie on your way over from Hattie Howard's place. Why?''

Dort stood behind the grandfather chair and watched the two dogs. ''I don't want that dog to go back to the shelter. My old dog is too near her end to be asked to share affection and space. I wondered if Chutney and Mag would get along.'' He winked at Tim. ''For today, they seem to be doing fine. Would you consider keeping her until Monday?''

That nice, peaceful little world I described to Jed is getting another jolt, Amy thought. But before she answered, she looked outside. Chut and Maggie lay sprawled in the sun, resting together with their noses touching.

"I can do that. For two days."

Dort crossed the kitchen and answered the phone before a second ring. He listened carefully and then covered the mouthpiece with his hand.

"It's Ruth Waldron. She's down at Allen's Point with Stanley's wife. That woman's story is a bit garbled. She's still sobbing but keeps saying she wants 'the dog.' Ruth thinks she's talking about Margaret. Says Rosabelle told her she has been looking for the dog, that Stanley hit her for asking about the dog and keeps repeating that Stanley took the nice, friendly dog. Ruth wants me to bring Margaret down there right away. She wants Stanley's wife to see this dog before the doctor arrives and gives her a shot to stop the sobbing and moaning. Amy, will you come with me?"

TWENTY-SIX

AMY AND DORT RODE in silence, busy with their own thoughts, until they passed the Morse Mill and Amy asked aloud, "Why there? Why was Stillman's body put in that shed?"

"Why was the dog tied up in Fullerton's barn? We asked that question. Maybe we have a partial explanation now. Stanley Waldron hated the Fullertons because they had him arrested for butchering their steers. By the way, he killed fifteen, took only the hind quarters, left the rest to rot. And those were prime steers, ready for market. He knew about the barn. Knew the house was empty. If he drove through Moose Corners on his way to Finley's Orchards, he'd pass the road to the farm. We may have another part of the answer if Stanley took Maggie away from Allen's Point because his wife liked the dog."

"Mean, meaner, meanest."

They rode in silence again for several miles before Amy said, "Bert Norton told me that after Stanley killed those steers, while the state police and sheriff's men were searching for him, he hid in that sawdust shed for a week. Maybe he thought it was a good place to hide a body?"

"Hang on to that thought until we talk with his wife. If she can or will talk, I'm hoping she'll be able to tell us something about Stanley's current activities," Dort said. "Hattie told us no one knew Stan's wife. Knows her. Did Stanley deliberately keep her isolated, away from people? Was it part of his nasty nature to keep a wife who doesn't drive or has no car in a house miles from town?"

"Do you suppose Rosabelle and Beaufort ever met and talked?" Dort asked. "Two lonely people. The only two on that part of the point during the day. We could build a story about those two."

A sad story, Amy thought. If you were alone and afraid, what did you do all day, every day? What did Beaufort do? What did women who were alone all day in isolated houses do during those hours? If a person didn't have a job, a passionate interest or an obsessive hobby, what would he or she do between breakfast and supper?

"I wonder where Stillman picked those tiny hemlock cones he had in his pocket," Amy said. "I stopped along here so Tim could see them growing. That candy wrapper hasn't been checked yet, has it? Of course not. You didn't take it until last night. My time sense isn't working. Too much has been happening too fast."

"Any more thoughts about your initial impressions when you first saw the body?"

"I remember asking myself if it was a Waldron boy," Amy said. "I was thinking of Ruth and Joe's boys. Stillman had that blond look. Not just his hair. A combination of hair and skin. What my father called 'fair Dutch.' But there was something else, something that hangs on the edge of my mind, just out of reach. When Carrie Parker told Tim that sad tale of sin in the fish house and the Henderson's webbed toes, I almost caught whatever thought or image keeps teasing my mind. Did the autopsy report note any physical oddities—warts or birth-marks? Anything unusual?''

"We're here," Dort said, and he turned into the gravel driveway where two cars were parked. "I think we're here before the doctor, but doesn't that station wagon belong to Arthur Waldron's wife?"

As soon as they stepped out of the truck, they heard the keening. What other word describes those sounds—the rising and falling of an empty, shrill, penetrating voice on the torn edges of grief and fear?

Before Dort could open the tailgate, Maggie sprang from the truck, ran to the door, and began whimpering and scratching. Dort didn't wait to knock. He opened the door and let Maggie in.

Ruth stood in the middle of the dark, drab room with her arms around a thin, wailing woman. Maggie pushed between the two and barked. Ruth loosened her arms and Rosabelle slid to the floor and buried her face in the thick black fur. Her sobbing ceased and her slender body relaxed, half over the big dog.

"Bless you both," said Ruth. "My guess was right. Look at that wonderful dog."

Maggie was lapping gently at Rosabelle's arm as the woman gathered the dog close and rocked back and forth, her keening silenced.

"What is that filthy dog doing in here? Who did this?" Arthur Waldron stopped halfway down the stairs.

Ruth moved in his direction. "Rosabelle was trying to tell me something about a dog Stanley took away so I asked Dort to bring Margaret down. See how this has quieted her?"

"When the doctor comes, he'll give Rosa a sedative so we can get her into an asylum or something. She's been out of her mind for years. Stanley was afraid an institution would cost him money. Now she will have to be put away." Arthur walked past Rosabelle and the dog and began to poke around on a high shelf where a non-functioning clock was surrounded by a pile of envelopes.

"Arthur," Amy's voice was low but firm. No one else spoke. She waited. Arthur turned, glanced at her briefly, then continued to finger the papers on the shelf. With his back to all of them, he asked, "What are you doing in my cousin's house?"

"Arthur, you and Stanley and Joe headed down the road from Granton to the harbor at the same time last Monday night. How long were you three together?"

"Mrs. Creighton, this is a house of sorrow. Only family, if you please." Arthur kept his eyes on the shelf. Did all Waldron men avoid eye contact? And reality?

Dort moved over beside Arthur and stood there, towering over him, almost touching. Dort was wearing brown corduroys, a faded plaid flannel shirt, and a new denim jacket. Arthur Waldron was, as usual, in his blue-gray "office suit," with a blue shirt and dark tie. His mud-caked shoes were the only false note in his neat accountant's appearance, his tidy, proper, businessman's dress.

No one spoke. Amy wanted to laugh and she suspected that Ruth was holding back a chortle. Dort seemed to get bigger and Arthur appeared to shrink. But no one made a sound. Stanley's wife was still on the floor with her face buried in Maggie's fur.

That's what Bentley Woodman saw when he came in. The door had been left ajar. Bent's deputy and two state police officers came in behind him.

Until Arthur, protesting quietly, went off with the sheriff, Rosabelle didn't seem to know or care what was going on around her. But after the officers' cars drove off and the house and yard were silent once more, she raised her puffy, blotched face and asked Ruth, ''Is Stan really dead? Is he going to stay dead?''

TWENTY-SEVEN

"LET'S MOVE OUTSIDE," Amy said. "This room is so dark and ugly it makes me feel cold and depressed. It's spring. The sun is shining. Let's go outdoors."

Dort spoke to Rosabelle in his gentle giant voice. "The dog needs to go outside. Will you come with us?"

"I'm not supposed to go out."

Ruth brought a cardigan sweater in from the back hall and put the big brown garment around Rosabelle's shoulders. She added her voice to Dort's. "The dog wants you to come with us."

The woman shivered and clutched the sweater around her. She looked frightened and confused. Dort opened the front door and called Maggie. The dog came to Dort but stopped in the doorway and whimpered. This sad sound drew Rosabelle to the door and, with her fingers clutching Maggie's fur and the dog close beside her, she followed Dort and Amy out onto the porch. Ruth, walking behind the worn-looking widow, gently guided her down the steps and along the weedy path.

The four moved from the shadow cast by the gray house across to the driveway into bright May sunshine. The warmth of this sunshine reflected from the boulders outlining the property and the metal of the three vehicles parked on the gravel.

Ruth kept her voice low. "What's the next step?"

"Coffee," said Dort. From the cab of his truck he brought out a thermos jug and four paper cups, handed them to Amy, and asked, "Will you pour?" From behind the driver's seat he pulled out a box of Girl Scout cookies and passed the open box to Rosabelle. Without looking at Dort, she took two cookies, fed one to Maggie, and popped the second one, whole, into her mouth.

Maggie sat, lifted her front legs, crossed her paws and let out a begging yip. Amy and Ruth laughed aloud. Dort grinned and Rosabelle reached for two more cookies.

"I told you she was a wonderful dog, didn't I?" Ruth directed her question to Amy. Then she turned to Rosabelle and asked, "Does she know any other tricks?"

Rosabelle set her coffee on the hood of Arthur's station wagon, made a clucking sound to the dog and then pointed her two index fingers toward the ground. Maggie promptly crouched low, head between her paws, belly and chin on the ground.

"She learned to be quiet so Stan wouldn't hurt her."

They drank their coffee and watched the dog, giving Rosabelle more time to relax, to warm up in the sunshine, and, perhaps, to speak to them before it was necessary to question her. Arthur had said, speaking in front of her, that Rosabelle needed to be "put away." Had she heard? Did she understand what he meant?

Dort continued to pass the cookie box until they finished the cookies and the coffee. Carrie Parker had spoken of Rosabelle as a "child." She was thin, a scrawny, half-starved thinness. Even her ears looked thin. Her eyes were red and puffy now from crying but the dark circles under those eyes gave them a sunken appearance.

Amy wondered how Rosabelle had heard about Stanley's death? Carrie said the woman was apparently alone, no cars in sight, when she and Jeb came on their neighborly visit.

Amy asked Ruth, "Arthur drove in after you arrived?"

"Yes. I came in through the cellar bulkhead around the back because the other doors were locked. Rosabelle knows me. But I couldn't calm her down. Arthur arrived just after I called you and Dort. I let him in and his presence upset her more."

Rosabelle knelt down beside Maggie and twined her hands in the dog's thick fur. She looked up at Ruth. "Arthur and Stanley want to get rid of me but they can't decide how to do it."

Dort moved over, sat on his heels on the other side of Maggie, and stroked the dog under her chin. "Does Arthur come here often?"

Rosabelle watched Dort's hands. "Arthur's afraid of Stanley." She was quiet for a moment and then looked up at Ruth. "Will Arthur still come even if Stanley is really dead?"

Dort answered, "If you don't want him to come, we'll see that he doesn't. Will it bother you to stay here alone?"

Rosabelle stared at Dort. "I'm always alone." As she spoke, Rosabelle cringed, appeared to shrivel, and buried her face again in Maggie's thick coat.

"Would you like this dog to stay with you?"

Rosabelle's body stiffened. They waited. Was she afraid of a trick or a trap? Of being the target of a cruel joke—being given hope and then having her hopes smashed and being laughed at? She lifted her head but didn't look up. "I would like the dog to stay." Silence. "Can she stay inside?"

"Maggie—we call this dog Maggie—has been lonely

and she has been hurt. She needs to be stroked and hugged.'' Amy spoke softly and watched Rosabelle's shoulders. "You used to hug her before Stanley took her away, didn't you?''

Rosabelle's thin shoulders hunched forward. She did not raise her face. "Stanley found me in the woods. Hugging the dog. So he took her away. In the truck. On Saturday.''

Dort's voice was kind and gentle. "Did you go into the woods looking for the dog?''

Amy held her breath. She felt that one false move, a wrong question or a raised voice, could send Rosabelle back to her keening, her pain and terror. How many years had Stanley Waldron kept this woman an emotional prisoner?

"He came after me,'' Rosabelle said. "I wasn't supposed to go out of the house and he brought the blond boy to sleep here and needed me to cook supper for them.'' She sat back on her heels and looked up at Dort. "Stanley started hitting me again because I couldn't stop crying. I wanted to find the dog.''

Dort reached out and gently patted Maggie. "Did the blond boy sleep here last Sunday night?''

"Yes. He was looking for a Waldron. Joe and Arthur came to help. Stanley locked me in my room.''

TWENTY-EIGHT

THE COLOR DRAINED from Ruth Waldron's face. Amy reached out and held her in a supportive hug until Ruth took a deep breath and lifted her head. "I don't want to believe any part of this. But Joe has been lying to me all week. And telling me I'm not a good wife because I question his stories." She looked from Amy to Dort. "Joe told me he came down here Sunday night to play poker. He acted surprised when we listened to the TV news and heard about the body in the sawdust shed. Waldrons stick together, he tells me. The family, always the family. And my sons are Waldrons."

Ruth turned away while she wiped her eyes and blew her nose and then she said, "I've got to get Doc's car back to him but Rosabelle can't be left alone. Shouldn't be left alone. Not in this mean, miserable house."

Amy and Ruth considered this angle of the situation while Dort spoke on the phone, relaying information to the sheriff. Rosabelle remained on her knees, her fingers still deep in Maggie's long hair and her face pressed against the dog's neck. That's how the doctor saw her when he pulled up behind Dort's truck. Henry Bradley, known on the peninsula as Dr. Hank, had given up his practice twelve years ago but he never drove away from home without his doctor's satchel. He spent a good part of his time visiting older folks, helping them understand

their illnesses, their doctor's orders, and how to fill out
the multiple insurance forms. Ruth had called Dr. Hank
because he lived in Granton and she needed immediate
advice on how to cope with Rosabelle's despair.

"Rosie, my dear, I'd like to pat that dog but my legs
won't let me get down there with you. Let's see if your
dog likes me."

Rosabelle sat back, looked up at Dr. Hank, and pulled
her hands free. Maggie got to her feet, sniffed the
satchel, and licked the doctor's hand. When Dr. Hank
leaned over to pat the dog's back, Maggie lapped Rosabelle's face.

Twenty minutes passed before the situation settled and
moved forward. Dort's car phone rang twice. Ruth maneuvered Doc Kelling's car around Emma Waldron's
station wagon and drove back to Granton. Dr. Hank said
he'd like Rosabelle to have about ten hours sleep before
he made further recommendations. She had symptoms
of shock but he felt this was more likely due to exhaustion and apprehension than a reaction to the news of her
husband's death.

Waldron men stick together. Ruth had said that several times. Hattie Howard had said it this morning. But
there didn't seem to be any Waldron women, or relatives, or close neighbors with whom Rosabelle could
stay. On this, her first day of widowhood, Rosabelle was
shamefully alone.

Amy, seeing no immediate alternative, told Rosabelle
that she wanted her—and the dog—to come to her house
to rest as Dr. Hank asked her to do, to stay overnight,
to sleep at Amy's house until tomorrow. She couldn't
tell how much Rosabelle understood. The woman appeared numb, in a state of shock, fear, and exhaustion.
Perhaps she was reacting to a long build-up of emotional

damage. Being locked in her room like a child. Being struck because she tried to find the dog, apparently the only creature that had shown her any affection in years. How many years? Rosabelle was, right now, locked in, walled in, incapable of normal responses.

After Dr. Hank left, Amy and Rosabelle waited for Dort and he waited for the police lab crew. Amy suggested a walk toward the shore. She didn't want to go back into that house. The two women walked slowly along the road but Maggie dashed off to explore the woods. Each time the dog went into the bushes, Rosabelle stiffened and cried out. Amy responded by putting an arm around the woman's thin shoulders and saying, "Wait." In a few minutes, the dog bounded back to the road, barked with pleasure, and raced off into the woods on the other side. They followed Maggie down Beaufort's driveway and found her resting in the large doghouse, head and paws outside, tongue hanging out. Amy located the dog's water dish and was looking for an outside faucet when Alex Beaufort came out.

Rosabelle stepped back and stood behind Amy, wrapping the big sweater around her. Maggie thumped her tail but made no move to come out to greet the man who had owned her. Amy spoke first. "We're taking a walk while waiting for the police to arrive." The mention of police startled Beaufort into a withdrawal similar to Rosabelle's hunched-over retreat.

Amy tried another way of explaining. "We've learned that the boy who was killed on Monday stayed here on the point Sunday night, at Stanley Waldron's house. The state police are on their way down here to check the house."

Amy turned to Rosabelle. "Do you know Alex Beaufort?"

"Will he take the dog?"

Beaufort looked at the big, black dog, resting in the door of the doghouse before he spoke to Rosabelle. "Would you like to have Margaret? To keep this dog?" Rosabelle responded with a bewildered stare so he turned to Amy. "She likes Margaret. Has ever since I brought the dog here. But she's afraid of me or she thinks I'm going to drive her away or something." He took the dog's water dish and filled it from a faucet beside the back steps.

"And you know what it's like to be afraid," Amy said. "Rosabelle has had several disturbing shocks recently and, right now, she's afraid this dog may disappear again."

Beaufort placed the water dish between Maggie's paws and the three of them watched her drink noisily. "You think Waldron took Margaret away?" he asked. "Is he the one who left the dog chained up with no water? That man is evil."

Amy watched Beaufort's face. "Someone killed that evil man last night."

"Killed him? He's dead?" Alex Beaufort's body relaxed. He stood straighter, looked taller, and almost smiled. "I should be sorry to hear someone died. But I feel relief. I'm glad that man won't come here anymore. He kept trying to borrow money. He thought I had money. Thought that I paid for this place. After Margaret disappeared, Waldron kept coming here and walking around the house. He even came knocking on the door in the middle of the night."

"Did you tell the sheriff about this when you reported prowlers?" Amy asked. "They came down here several times when you asked for help."

"No." Beaufort's eyes begged for understanding.

"No, I didn't. I wanted to but I didn't. I was afraid of what Stanley would do. He told me he was keeping an eye on me."

Dort's truck came down the slope of the driveway and he had to swerve and brake to avoid Maggie, who bounded out of the doghouse and almost slid under the wheels. Amy grabbed the dog's collar, pulled her back and held her while Dort turned the truck so it was headed out. When he let down the tailgate, Maggie hopped in and Rosabelle began to wail.

Amy opened the cab door, almost shoved Rosabelle inside, and told her to look out the rear window. Amy's voice was brusque. She explained that the dog liked riding in the back, that there wasn't room in the cab with three adults and Rosabelle could look back and see that Maggie was fine, resting happily. The wails ceased and Rosabelle huddled with her arms inside the big brown sweater. The dog, rescued on Thursday, was doing fine. How long would it take to rescue Mrs. Stanley Waldron? To help her begin to relax and respond to kindness?

Amy waited until Dort turned onto Harbor Road and they were headed back to Granton before she asked, "Did you find any evidence in the house? Anything to show Stillman had been there?"

"His keys and his wallet." Dort glanced at Amy's face. "And a return trip bus ticket—Boston to Buffalo."

TWENTY-NINE

AMY WANTED TO plump Rosabelle into a lawn chair in the sunshine and let the two dogs race around her. She wanted to flop onto a chaise lounge herself. But black flies had gathered on the back lawn and in every outdoor space.

Dort said, "Hot milk toast. With butter and salt. I'll fix it. She needs to eat, but something easy."

Rosabelle ate, looking into her bowl, with her left hand hanging over the arm of the chair. Maggie and Chut took turns licking that hand and arm. The woman expressed no curiosity about where she was. She showed no response to being in Amy's cheerful kitchen and didn't seem to notice when Dort, big, quiet Dort Adams, slipped a second bowl of hot milk toast in front of her. But as she finished that she said, "Dr. Hank wants me to sleep."

Amy led her down the hall, showed her the bathroom and the small room next to the office, and spread a soft pink blanket over the couch. Maggie sat on the rug and Rosabelle rubbed her cheek on the dog's head as she kicked off her shoes. When she clutched her sweater around her and curled up on the couch, Amy spread a blanket over her. Rosabelle seemed to fall asleep as soon as the soft blanket covered her.

Dort was spooning scrambled eggs onto two plates

when Amy came back to the kitchen. "Butter the toast while it's hot. Have any marmalade?"

"No marmalade. Raspberry jam. I had no idea I was so hungry." Amy set the cut-glass jam jar on the table and buttered the toast. They ate in silence until Dort got up to refill their coffee mugs.

He dropped his left hand onto Amy's shoulder as he poured her coffee. "Brain damage or a broken spirit? Is she one of the slow ones or does this kind of blankness happen if a person lives with someone like Stanley Waldron? That woman sees nothing except the dog. She's not here. She's off somewhere, like someone stoned."

Dort moved around to refill his mug. "But she was definite about the days and nights," he continued. "Stanley took the dog away on Saturday. The blond boy came Sunday night. Stanley began hitting her on Thursday. How can she appear so numb and dazed and shutdown and still tell us what happened on specific days? Can we trust she knows what she's talking about? I'd like to. Those times can help us check other evidence."

"Time, the organization of the week or names of the days are important to Rosabelle for some reason," Amy said. "Did she get some kind of reward on a certain day? Dread punishment on a particular day? Was she expected to cook certain meals on some days and needed to remember so Stanley wouldn't hit her? Maybe Ruth has some idea."

Amy looked up at Dort, who was standing beside the grandfather chair, holding the coffee pot, and said, "To whom did that poor woman talk—this week, last week, anytime? With whom? Not Stanley. You can't talk with someone who never listens. Has he been locking her in that awful house and yelling at her for more than ten

years? And no one knew or cared? Not even the other
Waldrons?''

"No one seems to have known William Stillman or
cared what happened to him," said Dort.

"Someone cared enough to kill him."

"We need to find the Waldron link," Dort continued.
"Find the Waldron listed as Stillman's father on his
birth certificate. Bent may have something on that by
now. His deputies told him there used to be Finnish families with that name in the western part of this county
and up Belfast way. He sent them looking for records—
an Olga Kouvalata listed in school, church, or voting
records twenty or twenty-two years ago."

They cleared the table and began washing up with no
need to discuss who was to do what. As Dort rinsed the
last bowl, he asked, "How many years did we do this
together?"

"Washing up was one thing we never argued about,"
Amy answered. "We just got at it and finished the job."

"Your sink is too low."

"For you. Not for me. Tell me what you think about
Arthur. Neat, tidy, polite Arthur who is a Waldron."
Amy went back and sat at the table, absently reached
for the cookie jar and began nibbling around the edges
of a big molasses cookie in the same way that Dort ate
around cookies.

"Sheriff Woodman took Arthur off for questioning,"
she said. "How does that work? Suppose he lies? What
do the police and the sheriff expect him to tell them?
That Arthur knew Stillman had been at Stanley's house
after he arrived in Maine? He withheld that information.
If Woodman confirms what Hattie told us—that Arthur,
Stanley, and Joe were together last Monday night before
Stillman's body was put into the sawdust shed—will Ar-

thur talk about it? Has anyone else offered evidence, come forward with any information, or is this strictly a Waldron muddle, the cousins who stick together?"

"Except for being Waldrons, what do those three have in common?" Dort leaned back in the big chair and munched around a cookie. He frowned and rubbed his left ear. Amy waited. "Stan's house is awful. I felt as though I was walking around in a collection of dump junk, carefully cleaned, no doubt one of Rosabelle's jobs. Junk spread around in drab, dark, cold rooms. The upstairs is as bad as that stark gray living room. Can you picture Stanley Waldron walking into Arthur's museum house? See Rosabelle and the gracious Emma getting together, visiting each other? We're missing something—missing whatever bonds those Waldrons together. Why was Arthur Waldron at Stanley's house Sunday night, the night Stillman was there?"

"We talked about a phone call Stillman might have made before he came to Maine or on his way to Granton that Sunday night," Amy said. "How many Waldrons are listed in the local phone directory? If Stillman called one of them, that one could have driven to pick him up where Granton Road meets Route One. Alphabetically, Arthur is the first Waldron name in the local directory."

Dort considered this. "Arthur's appearance would impress a stranger more than Stanley's. We're just guessing here but we do know Stanley could order his wife around while Arthur might have had a problem bringing home a stranger—bringing anyone into his clean, expensive, Christian home."

"I wish we could find the bag Stillman was carrying," Amy said. "Find the papers he told Tim he had stolen from his mother to help him look for 'family' in Granton. Do you think he still had that bag when he arrived at Stanley's house?''

Dort took another cookie while he considered Amy's question. ''Beaufort told you and the sheriff about Stanley being on his property looking for a bag, one he said he had lost. If Stillman recognized Stanley for the mean-minded bastard he is—he was—could the boy have hidden the bag to keep Stan from taking it, destroying it? But when could he do this after he arrived at Stanley's house?''

''Except...didn't Rosabelle tell us that Stanley came into the woods and brought her back to the house to cook supper?'' Amy asked. ''Stillman could have been alone for a few minutes. Or was Arthur already there? Was Joe there then? I wish Rosabelle was awake and responsive so we could ask her. Even if she was locked in most of the time, she must know something.''

THIRTY

CHUTNEY WHINED AT the door. Why was that other dog staying inside when there were chipmunks to chase, the pond shore to explore, and chicken bones to dig up where the camp folks had their barbecue?

Amy crossed the kitchen, let the dog in, and continued to speak to Dort. "Too many questions. Not enough answers. Why was Stanley Waldron prowling and poking around my house last night? What did he expect to find here?"

"Stan Waldron was here? Why didn't you tell me? Did you call the sheriff's office?" Dort raised his voice. "Tell me what happened."

Amy told him about Chutney's angry barking, of chasing the intruder out of the driveway and noting what appeared to be a broken taillight. Told him how, this morning, she saw that Stanley Waldron's truck, in Ira's driveway, had a similar broken taillight. Why hadn't she mentioned any of this? Because so much else was going on—finding Stanley dead, talking with Hattie Howard, the arrival of Sam Mozeson and Tim, and then Ruth's call for help. Too much happening without a breather, without catch-up time to review yesterday. Amy said she needed a few hours of solitude, time to think without interruptions.

"And if I had called you, what could you have

done?'' Amy asked. ''By the time you drove over here that truck would have been long gone. It went off too fast for me to try chasing it with my car. He, they, would have turned off and been out of sight before I could get my keys from the house. All I really saw was a difference in light intensity. The left rear taillight looked more white, less red.''

Amy shifted her voice from an angry tone to a quieter, softer level. ''Dort, if that was Stanley's truck, and I think it was, and if Stanley was the person prowling around here, then did Joe speed off to meet him after I called Ruth? Hattie told us she saw Joe's new truck go by her house last night after ten-thirty. And where was Arthur? He wasn't home when I called.''

''You called Arthur? When I called his house this morning to tell him we'd found Stanley's body, to tell him Stanley was dead, Arthur told me, volunteered the information, that he worked late last night, in his office. You called his home?''

''At ten-thirty at night, I wouldn't call his office. Of course I called his home. I was mad. My privacy had been invaded and I was hopping mad. So I called Arthur and hung up on his wife. I called Stanley's number and when no one answered there, I called Ruth. Joe was at home then. Maybe it was my call that sent him off into the night.'' Amy felt like stomping her feet. ''How can I tell you 'everything' when each time we start to talk and compare notes, we're interrupted? And what have you been holding back? What haven't you told me?''

''I'm the constable.''

''And I'm just a woman who happened to discover a body. A woman you used to know. Not important.''

''Amy, for God's sake, stop sounding like a frustrated adolescent. What do you want to know that I haven't told you? I asked you to let me talk with you about this case because you see things from angles I don't think of. You know facts and feelings about people I'm blind to. I wanted your help and you have been helping. I like working with you. I like you.''

"You like my cookies," Amy said, but she smiled as she spoke. "I'm edgy. I'm not sure how to cope with Rosabelle. She makes me think of those fragile glass globes that carnival men shatter with high-pitched sounds. But there's more.... I'm edgy because part of my mind keeps telling me I know something I don't know I know—something I can't catch."

Dort leaned against the sink and watched Amy pacing up and down the long kitchen. "You said that on Wednesday. Would it help to go back to where you first had that feeling? You know, like retracing your steps when you can't remember where you put your car keys when you came into the house and the phone was ringing?''

"It might. But I can't leave Rosabelle right now," Amy said. "June Kancapolos is back from Europe. She's driving up from Boston, will be here before six, and I haven't thought about supper. Tim and Sam are coming back. We shooed them out rather fast this morning and I need to talk with Sam. They're driving back to New York tomorrow.

"Dort, you said you talked with Lou Fullerton. Long distance or is she here? Did you tell her someone had been coming into the farmhouse, using the bulkhead entry? Did you ask her who stood in that little parlor and looked down to the old stone wall?''

"Lou is here. She and Graham Ford came last Saturday but they're staying up in Camden, waiting for some heating work to be done at the cottage." Dort moved over and opened the door to let Chutney back outside.

"They called me," he continued. "Lou and Graham want me to build a frame for one large painting and to discuss framing all the paintings they've brought for the exhibit they're doing in Camden in July. This will be their first joint exhibit in the east. I'll tell her you said to show that October painting."

"I'd like to own that," Amy said. "I can't get it out of my mind. But I'm not sure I'm brave enough or steady enough to live with it. To face, every day, what I see in that painting. I don't think I could deal with the feelings that painting stirs within me."

Dort stood in the doorway looking down toward the brook. "But you're glad you know those feelings."

"Yes. When I lifted the drape and first saw that October scene and when I see it again in my mind, I forget the rest—the hurts, the rejections, the death of what might have been."

They were both silent, standing apart, looking out into the bright spring sunshine, thinking their own thoughts of what had been and what might have been.

Dort's voice was low and he spoke slowly. "When Sally left, when she took my son and left a letter telling me what a failure I was as a husband, as a man, I swore I would never allow myself to go through that again. I'd back off. I'd be detached. I'd keep my distance. Seeing that October painting made me, makes me, want to feel again, to be fully alive once more."

Rosabelle's cries startled them and set Maggie howling. Amy rushed down the hall and held the woman's shoulders as her cries turned to screams. Dort lifted Maggie close to Rosabelle's hands and as soon as she grabbed the dog's fur, her voice quieted.

''Stanley wants to get rid of me. Arthur says he must get rid of me. I don't know what they're going to do but they're going to do it Sunday. After church. Please help me hide.''

THIRTY-ONE

MAGGIE SLATHERED Rosabelle's face with dog kisses. Amy sat with her arms around the trembling woman, rocking her back and forth, crooning, "It's all right. It's all right." Dort brought a wide-seated upholstered chair from Amy's office and lifted Maggie into it. With the front of the chair pushed against the narrow couch, Maggie could cuddle down with her body in the chair and her head on Rosabelle's pillow.

The screams quieted to sobs but Rosabelle continued to beg them: "Please help me hide." Amy's reassurance that she was safe went unheard.

Dort raised his voice and said firmly, "Maggie will protect you. Maggie will stay with you. The dog will not leave you." After a dozen repetitions, Rosabelle began to relax and, with her arm across Maggie's back, her fingers twined in the thick fur, she slipped off to sleep again.

Amy had tears in her eyes as she stood up and leaned into Dort, who rocked her as she had rocked the frightened woman. They held each other silently until Chutney came bounding in. Quietly, but prancing with pent-up energy.

"Someone's here."

Amy pulled the blanket over Rosabelle and followed Dort out into the hall. Bent Woodman and a taller, older man stood halfway down the hall, holding their hats in their hands. Dort waved them into the kitchen.

The sheriff turned to Amy, keeping his voice low. "I apologize for coming in but we heard the screaming...."

"Sit down." Amy indicated chairs around the oak table. "I'm glad you didn't interrupt or try to interfere." She took a seat at the long table and the three men joined her. "Dr. Hank wants Rosabelle, Stanley's wife, to sleep. He thinks her state of shock is partly due to exhaustion. You heard her screams. She's more than frightened. I think she's been a prisoner in that house so long she's out of her mind. She's afraid of what's going to happen next. Needs rest before you or anyone attempts to question her. Right now, the only thing that calms her is that dog."

This time Bentley Woodman had not interrupted her. He looked at Dort. "The dog that was left to die in the Fullerton barn?"

Dort nodded.

Shaking his head at this information, Sheriff Woodman nodded at his companion and said, "This is John Jones, state police detective. Amy Creighton and Dort Adams. John's following up on the lab crew's findings and wanted to talk with both of you."

"John Jones?" Amy said, looking startled.

Jones smiled. "I'm used to such reactions. I've also had years of listening to remarks about the names of my cousins—Zachary, Faustina, Danae, and Claudius. Plain John is easier to say and spell." He looked at his notebook and frowned before he said, "We do need to question Mrs. Waldron but I'm sure you're right about waiting. We heard her screams. Do you need help while she's here? A nurse?"

"I haven't thought that far ahead," Amy said. "Right

now it seems most important to make her feel safe enough so she can and will sleep. I don't think she has any relatives in this area, any family, except Ruth Waldron. Ruth's a nurse but she has her job, the two boys, and her husband...." Amy paused and looked at the sheriff. "Have you questioned Joe?"

John Jones answered. "Joe and Arthur Waldron have both been questioned. Are still being questioned. Their stories don't match but they've both admitted to withholding information. Both of them told us they talked with William Stillman at Stanley's house Sunday night but say they didn't see the victim on Monday."

Dort asked, "What have you learned about Stanley's wife? Who was Rosabelle before she married Stanley and where did he find her? Does she have any family?"

Bentley flipped several pages in his notebook. "Nasty story. According to a couple of men who did time with Waldron, he bought Rosabelle. She was fifteen at the time. Her brother wanted to leave the state and needed cash. The only thing he had to sell was his sister. Name was Dupre. From a farm up north of Lewiston. The brother insisted on a legal marriage and then he left. We haven't located him yet."

Amy looked at Dort. "Joe and Arthur must have known this. Joe acts like a dim brain, a selfish, dim brain, but Arthur plays the proper gentleman, solid citizen, a leader in his church. He must have known Rosabelle's background and known that she was a prisoner. For years. He's as evil as Stanley. More evil. Stanley never pretended to be a nice person. This morning Arthur accused me of invading a house of sorrow. How right he was!"

Dort asked the state police detective if he had more information on Stillman's adoption and the birth parents.

"We followed up on the suggestions Mrs. Creighton gave the sheriff's office and checked newspaper files for the feature stories she wrote years ago on Finnish families in this part of Maine." Jones looked at Amy. "Mrs. Creighton's memory of her features was accurate. There was an Olga Kouvalata. Still is, but now she's Olga Walker. On the date given on the birth certificate for the baby the Stillmans adopted, Olga Kouvalata was down in Texas with a tour group, birding on Padre Island—something she wanted to do and her fiancé didn't. Mrs. Walker thinks someone who knew she would be out of state, someone who wanted to keep the baby's birth a secret, used her name. Gave her name at the admissions desk."

"Maybe the mother died?" Amy suggested. "Does Olga Walker have any idea who might have used her name?"

"Told us she didn't," John Jones said. "When we asked if she knew any Waldrons, Mrs. Walker told us that in high school she and Jennie Waldron, Arthur's sister, had been friends but she knew Arthur and his brother Carl only by sight."

"Paul Arthur. Paul Arthur Waldron. Named for his mother Pauline." Amy looked from Jones to Dort. "Hattie Howard told me that Parker Waldron named his son for his wife Pauline. I didn't make the connection then. Paul Arthur. That P. A. Waldron on the birth certificate could be Arthur. The link to William Stillman. I only half heard Hattie this morning because I was trying to get her to tell me about the trucks and cars she saw passing her house Monday night and last night."

Dort spoke to Amy as though Jones and Woodman were not there. "If Emma knew Arthur was the father of a baby, she never would have married him."

"If he didn't marry Emma Ramsdorff, he couldn't buy and live in the old Gregg place."

Dort responded, "A man with an illegitimate child couldn't marry Emma Ramsdorff and become a church leader—not in that East Granton church."

"But who was the mother?"

"If the baby was born in March, why hurry the Stillmans out of town in October?" Dort asked. "What else was going on?"

Amy followed through on what her father used to call their "verbal volleyball." "When did Parker Waldron drown off Bean Island with his head bashed in?" She lifted her hand to halt the conversation for a moment. "How close are the dates of the baby's birth, Olga's trip to Texas, Parker's death, and the Stillman's move out of town? Yes, and Arthur's marriage?"

Dort looked from the sheriff to the detective. "Does Arthur's sister live near here? She might recall other events around the time of her father's death. Is Pauline Waldron still living? Hattie said that Parker Waldron's family lived up in Rockland."

Woodman and Jones checked their notes. "William Stillman's birth certificate says he was born in Augusta in March 1979 and the adoption records are dated October 1979, just before they left Maine. Mrs. Walker was in Texas during the first three weeks of March that year. Where was the baby from March until October?" The police detective asked Dort and Amy, "Do you have any reason to believe the time of the Stillmans' move out of state was connected with the adoption that month?"

Amy stood and moved toward the hall. "I'll use my office phone to call Carrie Parker and ask about Arthur's sister and mother. Probably the quickest way to get information on Saturday." She pointed to the wall phone by the kitchen door and said, ''If your men are still questioning Joe and Arthur, you might call in, see if they will give you straight answers. Ask about P. A. Waldron and Arthur's mother.''

Carrie listened to Amy's questions and her reasons for needing information right then. Parker Waldron's body was found on the shore of Bean Island in September 1979. Family had a double funeral for him and his daughter, Jennie, who died the same week. Parker was on Bean Island visiting a woman he had been visiting for years. Pauline Waldron was in one of those nursing homes out toward Augusta. Arthur's brother, Carl, the bright one, lives in Virginia. Never comes home. Carrie told Amy to ask Dr. Hank about the Waldrons. He could tell her about the foul play rumors when Parker drowned and about the stories told when Jennie died. Poor girl was so young.

''It's like uncovering a cesspool, a leaking septic tank,'' Amy said after she relayed Carrie's answers to Woodman and Jones. ''You can send someone to the nursing home to talk to Pauline. Dr. Hank must know which home it is and can probably tell you whether her mind is clear enough to answer questions. It would be quicker to ask Arthur but he seems to have forgotten how to tell the truth.''

Amy walked to the door with the two law men. ''I'm going to call Ruth, Joe's wife. I don't want to believe that she knew how Stanley treated Rosabelle. But she must know something.''

Woodman and Jones moved off to their cars. The state police detective called back, ''We'll keep in touch. If you need help, phone. We'll swing over to East Granton now and talk with Dr. Hank before we speak with Emma

Waldron. As soon as you can do it without upsetting her, find out if Rosabelle knows when Stillman left Stanley Waldron's house—whether he walked out or was carried.''

THIRTY-TWO

"YOU'RE AS TENSE AS an overwound top. Come outside and stretch while I rewrite my list of unanswered questions." Dort took Amy's hand and led her through her office to the narrow porch.

Amy stretched and counted. Chutney came down across the back lawn and settled beside Dort. He rubbed the dog's head and scratched under her chin while he studied the notes on the small pad he carried in his shirt pocket.

"Did I laugh at you when you said you thought the abuse of the dog and the boy's death were connected?"

"And the lights up at the Fullerton farm on Monday night. You didn't laugh at my feelings but you let me know, quite definitely, that you viewed those three as separate happenings," Amy said. "The car lights up there may not be important but they need to be explained. Whoever was on that hill Monday night saw and heard Maggie."

Dort considered this and looked at his notes again before he answered. "On Monday night, whoever killed Stillman was probably looking for a place to dump the body. Unless your wheelbarrow idea explains that. Rosabelle said Stanley took the dog away from Allen's Point. If he chained Maggie in the Fullerton's barn, and he was the one up here on Monday night, he saw and heard the dog. Knew the dog was suffering but didn't give her food or water. Wicked. Evil. Why didn't the man just shoot her? He carried guns in his pickup.''

"He did? Didn't his record prohibit his carrying a gun?''

"Stanley applied for a permit to carry a gun, guns, when he went to work at Finley's Orchard. He shot porcupines that girdled the trees and woodchucks that ate the young plants. We found a rifle and a pistol in his truck this morning. Both loaded.'' Dort ran his finger down the page of notes and asked, "Did you get the feeling Rosabelle knew Dr. Hank?''

"He called her Rosie but that could be his way of calming her,'' Amy pointed out. "When she finished that hot milk toast she told us Dr. Hank wanted her to sleep. As though his words were important to her.''

Dort looked up at Amy. "If he'd treated her before, wouldn't he know she was being abused? And that brings me back to the question of whether the woman is retarded, not too bright, or whether her blankness is a result of living with Stanley and being isolated from other people.''

Amy stepped down and shook out her shoulders but before she could answer, Chutney barked and raced around the house and up to the driveway. "It's probably Sam and Tim. I don't want them to wake Rosabelle.''

She went into the house through the office. Dort followed Chutney up the lawn to the driveway. They both signaled for silence when they met Sam Mozeson and Tim at the front door.

In the kitchen, keeping their voices low, Dort and Amy brought the Mozesons up to date on what had happened since the two of them had rushed off to Allen's

Point. Told them about Rosabelle's responses to Maggie, her need to rest before the doctor saw her later in the day. Before the state police came back to question her.

Tim told them he had driven his father to Sacaja Harbor, introduced him to Carrie and Jeb Parker and showed him Beaufort's cottage. They had seen a police car at the gray house Dort had told them was Stanley Waldron's but no other activity along that road. And they had some news.

"My father wants to buy Beaufort's place if it comes up for sale," Tim said. "My father, the city man who has never even walked across Central Park, thinks he wants to look at the Atlantic Ocean from the rocky shores of Allen's Point."

Sam Mozeson nodded to confirm Tim's statement, to acknowledge the strangeness of this impulse. "I think I was ten years old the last time I suddenly wanted something very much, had an overwhelming desire for something. It was a puppy, a round, brown-and-white spaniel puppy. I knew I couldn't have it. My family liked things tidy and sterile. But, if Beaufort or his mother decides to sell, I can have that cottage. If I discover, later, that I'm not comfortable being close to the sea, isolated on a Maine peninsula, at least I'll know that I indulged myself. I'll know that I had an impulse and acted on it."

Amy looked across the table at her editor, neat and well barbered, professional down to his buffed fingernails, and wondered how he'd look after a hike along that rocky shore or a clam bake on the point. After working with the man for eight years, knowing him only through his voice and the ideas exchanged during weekly editorial conversations, Amy liked the idea of having Sam Mozeson as a neighbor during the time he would spend in a cottage on the coast.

"If you allow anyone else in your office, perhaps we can work together while I'm here in Granton." Then Sam told Amy, "Last week I purchased a manuscript on building a new life after personal tragedy. Bought it because I was struck by the nature observations. Nature in Maine. This one is just right for you to edit. Then maybe you can show me where I might see beavers building shelters and dams, where I could watch loons dance in the moonlight."

Tim said he and his father were heading back to Westport Island and planned to leave early the next morning for New York. But they would both be coming back to Granton.

THIRTY-THREE

"WHEN I CHECK IN with Bent, he'll have six things for me to do. How can I help you before that?" Dort sat on his heels beside the driveway as he rubbed Chutney's ears.

Amy brushed the flies away from her face. "The asparagus needs to be cut but I don't want to be out of calling distance from Rosabelle. It would help if you'd cut or stay in with her while I do it."

"Give me a knife. My skin's tougher than yours."

Amy watched Chutney follow Dort from the kitchen door to the asparagus patch on the far side of the back lawn. The green spears now ready to be cut were growing on the same sunny knoll beyond the pond path where she and Dort had set in the first roots as a high school science project. The bed was larger now. Years of adding compost, of cultivation and annual mulching, had raised the level of the soil but Dort was harvesting from the roots or, rather, the offspring of the roots the two of them had planted all those years ago. And argued over. Dort read that salt spread along asparagus rows would inhibit weeds but Amy's earth science courses warned about the long-range effects of salts, how they could damage soil structure.

But if we hadn't argued about chemical changes in soil composition and texture, Amy said to herself, we

would have disagreed about something else. She began
to take supper supplies from the freezer. The package of
Chinese pork brought back memories of summers in
Granton during college years and the verbal battles about
garlic that she and Dort had kept going for weeks. Did
garlic have medicinal value in preventing colds and improving blood circulation or were those just old wives'
tales? The loaf of onion and walnut bread recalled disagreements about adding ground nuts to puddings,
breads, and meat loaves. Adding nuts to foods that
shouldn't have nuts in them. Sounds of old arguments
swirled through her head. When Dort came in with the
asparagus, Amy was laughing aloud at the memory of a
loud-spirited discussion they had the night she added
ground peanuts, tomato paste, and molasses to a venison
meat loaf.

"Care to share? Something struck your funnybone."

"Ground peanuts in a venison meat loaf. Remember
that argument? Didn't we have anything more important
to occupy our minds?" Amy asked. "All that energy
wasted on trying to be right about garlic or peanuts—
major issues. And your wanting to pour salt around the
asparagus plants. Was that first planting your project or
mine?"

"Mine. There was no sunny space in back of our
house and my mother was adamant about keeping the
front yard pure, the way front yards were supposed to
look. She reacted to my idea of planting asparagus in
front of the house by lapsing into one of her over-
wrought, muttering, moaning scenes. She had that act
practiced to perfection. That was the way she took on
when I told her we wanted to canoe through Sacaja Pond
and down the river to the harbor."

"Did she ever find out that we did?"

"I don't think so. I learned not to talk, not to mention what I was thinking about or doing in order to avoid having to listen to her moanings. My father and the neighbors did the same. We had a conspiracy not to tell my mother anything that might set her off." Dort washed and dried his hands, helped himself to a cookie and asked, "Anything else I can do before I call in?"

"Thanks, Dort. I think I'm all set. I hope Rosabelle will keep on sleeping. Maybe I'll call Doc Kelling's office and see if Ruth is still there." They walked down the hall and as Dort opened the screen door, Amy asked, "Does it seem odd to you that Dr. Hank didn't give Rosabelle a sleeping pill? Or suggest any such medication if she didn't calm down?"

"I wondered about that. Doctors usually do give sleeping pills to women."

"I'm not talking about 'women.' I'm talking about one particular human being who's tired and tense and frightened. And I've never put Dr. Hank in the same class as those me-and-God know-everything doctors who treat women as though they were weak-minded, second-class, unimportant citizens. But I do wonder if Dr. Hank knows something about Rosabelle. Maybe she has allergies, drug reactions. Something we don't know that made him recommend sleep first. Just sleep."

Dort rubbed his left ear. Amy waited. He said, "I'm going to call Dr. Hank. Now."

Dort came back around the truck. "You're right. Dr. Hank says that because Stanley gave pills to Rosabelle, she's now frightened at even the sight of a pill. He thinks Stanley sometimes drugged her so she'd stay inside while he was away. Said he had reported this but needed proof. He'll be by later to see how you're doing. I'll be back as soon as I can."

Chutney followed Amy down into the cellar. The dog sniffed at the old stone foundation while Amy brought jars of applesauce and strawberry jam out from the storeroom. Suddenly, Chutney dashed up the stairs and began to growl, low, angry growls. Amy followed and found Chut crouching in the front hall, holding Emma Waldron at bay between the front door and the door into the kitchen. The woman must have just walked in because Chutney would have responded to knocking or the sound of the old bell.

"Mrs. Creighton, please call this dog away. I've come to get Rosabelle. Arthur wants her at our house."

THIRTY-FOUR

AMY WALKED TO Emma Waldron and around her, toward the front door. As she passed the large woman, standing in the middle of the wide hall, she said, "Quiet, please. Come this way. Outside."

Only Emma's head moved. She stood with her feet apart, looking both formidable and threatening. She repeated, "I've come to get Rosabelle."

Amy put the jars she was carrying down on the hall table and lowered her voice to a whisper. "Please be quiet, Mrs. Waldron. Dr. Hank wants Rosabelle to sleep."

Chutney held her place, blocking the hall, and she continued her growling, ready to pounce. Emma Waldron didn't attempt to walk past the dog but neither did she seem to be afraid. And she did not lower her voice. "Get that dog out of here. Arthur wants me to bring Rosabelle to our house."

"Will you please shut up!" Amy wanted to drag the woman out of her hallway but Emma Ramsdorff Waldron was a mountain of a woman, taller, wider, and heavier than Amy. "Rosabelle has suffered several shocks. She's exhausted. She's just settled down. She needs rest."

"She can rest at our house. Arthur wants her there."

"Arthur can wait. Have the police finished question-

ing him and Joe?'' Amy waited for some kind of response, but Emma just stood, feet apart like bridge struts
to support her heavy body. Her face remained expressionless as though she hadn't heard the question. Amy
didn't want to command Chutney to bite—yet. So she
stepped back, looked up at Emma, and asked, "Did Arthur tell the sheriff that the murdered boy was his son?"

Emma heard that question. She looked down at Amy
and shook her head. "Arthur doesn't have a son. We
have no children. Arthur doesn't know that boy from
Buffalo. What kind of lies are you and the police making
up?"

Chutney barked, once, and bared her teeth.

Amy gestured toward the front door. She did not want
this woman in her kitchen. Did not want to talk with her
inside the house. Emma turned and took several steps
toward the door but then repeated, "Arthur wants me to
bring Rosabelle to our house."

Through the screen door Amy could see the Waldron's station wagon backed up to the front steps with
the rear door open and a folded quilt on the floor. Had
Emma intended to sling skinny Rosabelle over her
shoulder and plunk her into the car like a sack of potatoes? Haul her off like trash?

When Emma finally stepped outside, Amy leaned
against the door with her hand on Chutney to calm the
dog and to give herself more confidence. "Sheriff
Woodman will be here shortly. He and the state police
have more loose ends to check. Does your husband only
use his full name—Paul Arthur—or P. A. Waldron on
official papers?"

Emma looked more confused than angry but she
slammed the rear of the station wagon shut. Chutney
gave a warning growl. Amy held the dog's collar as

Emma Waldron glared at them, fists clenched at her sides. Then she moved around to the driver's side. When the station wagon circled the bend in the lane and was out of sight, Amy sat down on the steps and buried her face in Chutney's neck.

She was still trembling when she felt Chutney's muscles tighten and Amy fell backward as the dog sprang off the steps and dashed toward the garden house just below the garage. Joe Waldron stepped from behind the building wielding a piece of lumber as a club and before Chutney could attack, Joe knocked the dog senseless in the driveway.

Joe Waldron moved toward her swinging the oak club. Amy sensed his anger. With his next blow he could drop her as he had Chutney. Part of her mind calculated paths to safety, places to hide, but a stronger part directed her to move away from the house so Joe would follow her and not get near Rosabelle. As she ran down the slope toward the pond path, Amy heard her phone ringing. On the far side of the bridge, Amy grabbed at the rotten posts and tipped two of them down across the path. Before she reached the pond shore, she heard Joe's cursing as he fell over them.

Into the pond. Swim underwater. Get around behind the big rock, out of sight. Panic spurred her on and Amy was neck deep in the cold water, behind whale rock, trying to breathe quietly when Joe came out of the woods yelling and swearing and pounding his club against the boulders. "You nosy old bitch. I'll get you. You show your head and I'll smash it. Stay under water. Stay down there and drown, you nasty old biddy!"

Would the ripples on the pond surface lead him to her? Or was the man too riled to think?

Joe was still yelling when Amy heard an angry growl,

followed by a scream and splashing. She raised her head to peer around the rock and her heart gave a leap of joy. That blow to the head had not killed Chutney. It seemed to have intensified the dog's protective instincts. Chut was on top of Joe, who had toppled face first into the pond. The man's head was under water and Chutney was not letting him up. Amy swam around to shallow water and, when she saw that Joe's arms and legs had stopped moving, she commanded Chut to back off. She lifted the man's face out of the water.

Chutney's bark warned her to look back. Arthur Waldron emerged from the path. Neat, tidy Arthur in his blue-gray suit. He looked unmoved, unwrinkled, unperturbed by anything that had happened this day, since his cousin's body had been found at dawn. Was the man totally devoid of feelings?

"What have you done to Joe?"

"He tried to attack me. He may have swallowed too much water. Help me turn him over."

"I'll go call the fire department." Arthur turned and almost ran back up the path. And ran straight into John Jones, who brought him back to the shore.

Joe began heaving and coughing up water as soon as Arthur and Amy turned him over. Jones lent a hand and they pulled Joe up onto the beach so he was on his side. The detective cleared an area in the sand for his face. The black flies clustered first on the wet faces and then sought blood from Jones and Arthur.

Chutney's barks were answered by more barking as Maggie and Rosabelle emerged from the path. Chut pranced around Maggie. Rosabelle clutched the oversized sweater more closely around her and looked from Arthur to Joe and then to Amy.

"You're wet. Your clothes are wet."

"I've been in the pond," Amy said. "The flies down here are terrible. Let's get back to the house." She picked up the oak two-by-four Joe had used as a club and spoke to John Jones. "How can I help?"

"Get Rosabelle inside. Lock the doors and stay there until Woodman and Adams arrive. They're on their way. Let me keep that wood. I may need it."

Amy spoke to the dogs and started to shepherd Rosabelle up the path but the woman turned to speak to Arthur. "You told Stanley to get rid of me on Sunday. Stanley's dead. Really dead. He can't get rid of me. Are you going to do it?"

Arthur spoke to John Jones. "That woman is out of her mind. She should have been locked up years ago."

Rosabelle retreated from the venom in Arthur's voice but moved backward too quickly, fell over Maggie, and spread out both arms to stay her fall. The bulky sweater slipped from her shoulders and a canvas bag dropped to the ground. Arthur lunged for it but Jones whomped him on the rump with Joe's club. Arthur Waldron sprawled across the beach with his face in the sand. Amy grabbed the bag.

THIRTY-FIVE

BOTH DOGS LIFTED their heads as a strong whistle sounded from beyond the path, but neither bounded off in response. Maggie's tail thumped faster but she stayed close beside Rosabelle, who was still on the ground, huddled again into the big brown sweater. Chutney's ears pricked up and she waved her wet tail but remained on guard between her mistress and Joe Waldron. Amy smiled, lifted her head, and answered with a high whistle.

"It's Dort," she said to John Jones. "We whistle to locate each other."

Arthur knelt on the beach, wiping sand from his face and hands with a linen handkerchief. Joe retched and coughed and struggled to raise his head and shoulders from the sand and crawl away from the edge of the pond. Dort charged out of the woods so fast he almost fell over Arthur as he reached both hands to Amy.

"Are you all right? You're not hurt?"

"Safe and wet. And shaky." Amy leaned against Dort for a moment and then held up the canvas bag. "Arthur wanted it. Rosabelle had it. But I don't know why Joe was after me."

Rosabelle said, "Arthur knows."

John Jones waved his hat at the swarms of black flies, wiped blood away from the bites around his eyes, and

asked Amy to take Rosabelle back to the house. Said he
and Dort would be along as soon as they had Joe on his
feet. Dort lifted Rosabelle and steadied her until Amy
had the two dogs headed up the path. Maggie followed
Chutney and Rosabelle followed Maggie.

Back inside the kitchen, Amy settled the silent woman
into an armchair at the table and used the microwave to
make a cup of tea. She locked the three doors as Jones
had requested but thought it was probably unnecessary
now. She put a slice of buttered bread beside Rosabelle's
sugared tea—she had cut the slice into small strips as
her grandmother had cut bread in order to coax a tired
child to eat just a bit. When Rosabelle began to eat, Amy
slipped into the laundry room to remove her wet clothes.
She listened for sounds from the kitchen as she put on
a terry robe.

On impulse, Amy took a soft blue cardigan from the
drying rack and asked Rosabelle to exchange the bulky
brown sweater, still wrapped around her, for the blue
one. It was like dressing a sleepy child. Rosabelle didn't
mind giving up the ugly old sweater and once her arms
were in the sleeves of the blue one, a change occurred.
She lifted her head, looked directly at Amy and said, ''I
wore a dress this color when I was married.'' She rubbed
her hands down each arm and added, ''I like blue.''

A knocking at the front door set both dogs barking.
Maggie stood up but remained beside Rosabelle. Chut
raced down the hall and stood guard as Amy directed
the officers around to the pond path.

''Are we locked in?'' Amy found Rosabelle standing
behind her as she turned after closing the front door and
locking it again.

''Yes. But we can unlock the doors if we want to. We
need to be careful until the police know more about

what's going on." Amy watched Rosabelle's face, looking for a response to her words but the woman's expression remained blank.

"Come upstairs with me. I need to get dressed."

Rosabelle followed Amy up to her bedroom and stood
beside the bed, silent and docile. Chutney flopped down
on her sleeping rug and Maggie moved about, sniffing
and snuffling in all corners of the room. But when Amy
slid the closet doors open, Rosabelle uttered a cry of
pleasure.

"Someday I'm going to have a closet and pretty
clothes. And every day I'm going to open my closet and
look and feel and decide what to wear. Someday."

Amy held her breath, not wanting to interrupt. She
took out a hanger holding a floral print skirt in wild
tropical colors and laid it on the bed. Rosabelle ran her
fingers over the print and said, "A green top with this."

When Amy pulled open a drawer holding jerseys, she
stepped back and watched Rosabelle look from the skirt
to the colored tops in the drawer. "This one. With a
gold necklace. Maybe a gold chain."

And then, as suddenly as she had responded to the
clothes, Rosabelle retreated. She cringed and stepped
back as though she expected to be struck.

Amy placed the top Rosabelle had chosen on the bed
beside the skirt. She took a triple strand gold necklace
from her jewelry box, put it on top of the green jersey,
stood back and asked, "Will that one do?" She lifted a
rope of gold and purple beads and placed that beside the
gold chains. "Or would this be better?"

Rosabelle reached out, lifted the bright rope, and let
it slide over her fingers. When she held it up against her
face, tears slid down her cheeks. "The summer people
throw away magazines with pictures of clothes and jew-

elry. I take them out of their trash when no one is looking. All winter I can look at lovely things.''

Her face changed back to blankness. Amy, watching
the shifts in Rosabelle's expressions and voice, was reminded of electrical brownouts, the weakening of electrical power on country lines. As lights dim, beaters slow
down, recorded music becomes fainter, and one holds
one's breath. Will the lights go out? And, if there's a
surge as full power returns, will it blow a fuse? Maggie
seemed to serve as a power cushion, a battery of reserve
power. The dog moved in closer each time she sensed
that Rosabelle's energy level was falling lower. When
the woman's hands were twined in the dog's long hair
she gained strength.

Rosabelle dropped the rope of beads onto the bed.
"Stanley found my magazines and made me burn them.
One by one. All of them.''

Rosabelle had not only been a prisoner in that dark,
ugly house, Stanley had ferreted out all the things that
gave her pleasure and destroyed them. Except Maggie.
She had been rescued. Why, with all the good people in
Granton and Sacaja Harbor, had no one rescued Rosabelle? That Maine live and let live ethic. Don't interfere.
If Rosabelle had run down the road screaming while
someone was driving by, her needs might have been
noticed. But probably, even before he brought her to
Granton, to that isolated house, Stanley's meanness had
frightened the child and destroyed her spirit.

Amy dressed quickly, choosing the triple gold chain
to wear with the green top and print skirt and then she
took a string of blue beads from her dresser top case and
put them into Rosabelle's hands. She watched the young
woman's face relax before asking, "Did the blond boy

go away on Monday morning or did he stay in your house all day?''

Rosabelle fingered the beads as though each was a pearl of great value and, keeping her eyes on them, she said, ''Arthur took him away in the morning. Stanley gave me pills to make me sleep but I didn't swallow them so I saw them leave.''

Which question next? At any moment the sheriff and the police would be coming up from the pond. How did Rosabelle get Stillman's bag? Did the boy leave willingly with Arthur?

''Arthur took the blond boy away Monday morning. Did the boy want to go with Arthur?''

''Arthur told him he'd take him to meet P. A. Waldron. So the boy went with him.''

Amy's bedroom windows overlooked the back lawn and the bridge over the stream. Both women turned toward the windows as footsteps sounded on the wooden bridge. John Jones and Arthur came across and up the path, a rumpled Arthur with wet shoes, wet pant legs. Dort followed with one of the taller deputies, helping Joe stumble along. Bentley Woodman followed along with his other deputy and two police officers.

Rosabelle quickly handed the blue beads to Amy and backed away from the window. Maggie whined. Chut raced down the stairs to guard the door. Amy slipped the blue beads over Rosabelle's head and turned her to the mirror. Then, as she tied the laces of the sneakers she had put on, Amy asked, ''Do you want to stay up here? I have to go down to answer the door.''

That lost, dazed look came over Rosabelle's face again. She sat in the corner chair, twined her fingers in Maggie's fur, and whispered, ''Don't let Arthur in. Keep him away from me. Please.''

"Arthur will not enter my house. I promise you."

Dort was waiting at the front door. He stepped inside, gathered Amy in his arms, and held her without speaking until the sheriff knocked.

"We need to look in that bag," Dort said. He opened the door for the sheriff and John Jones and then asked, "Is Rosabelle OK? We'd like to ask her about the bag."

"Check the bag first," Amy said. "Dr. Hank may be along soon. I don't want anything to make her slip back into that state of shock. She's on the brink. Please wait."

Amy had tossed the knapsack onto the kitchen counter when they came in from the pond. Her priorities then were to lock the doors, calm Rosabelle, and get out of her wet clothes. The detective opened the canvas bag and spread a handful of papers out on the long oak table.

Dort held one rumpled paper down with both hands, read through it, and looked up at Amy, who was standing in the doorway, listening for sounds from upstairs.

"Motive," said Dort. He looked from to Amy to Woodman to Jones. "William Stillman was the child of Paul Arthur Waldron and his sister, Jennie. That filthy, lying hypocrite."

THIRTY-SIX

BENTLEY WOODMAN held up two newspaper clippings. "Double funeral for Parker Waldron and his daughter, Jennie," read one. "Parker Waldron's body with smashed skull found among rocks on Bean Island. Sheriff investigating." Woodman looked at Jones. "Both clippings are from October, just before the Stillmans moved away."

"Jennie died just before the Stillmans left with the baby and Arthur married Emma Ramsdorff. This happened right here in Granton and nobody knew."

"Somebody knew," John Jones said. "Several somebodies. Woodman, let's have the officers take them both in now. Arthur for suspicion of murder. Joe for aggravated assault. I have more questions for Dr. Hank but I'd like him to see these papers first."

Amy asked, "May I call Ruth? So she'll know where Joe is, what's going on?"

"I'll call," Dort said.

"What about Emma, Arthur's wife?" Amy asked. "I've had no chance to tell you. She was here, came on Arthur's orders, to get Rosabelle. Had the back of her station wagon open, ready to load the poor woman in like a bale of peat moss."

"We'll talk to her again," Jones said. "She must have driven over here as soon as Arthur got home. He was

taken back to Allen's Point to pick up the station wagon
after the questioning. We need to talk with the Stillmans.
Both of them. Not their lawyer.''

Sheriff Woodman folded the papers carefully back
into William Stillman's canvas bag and the two men
went out to speak to the deputies and state police in the
driveway. Amy looked out from the front hall door. Law
officers watched from each side of the Waldrons. Woodman and Jones stopped to talk beside the first police car.
Arthur stood behind the station wagon and Joe leaned
on that car, pressing his forehead against the curve of
the roof, both hands spread out beside his head. Amy
turned quickly and bumped into Rosabelle, who had
come quietly downstairs and was staring at the men in
the driveway. Amy grabbed Rosabelle's right hand and
lifted it up.

With her left hand, Amy held the tip of Rosabelle's
little finger and moved it back and forth. ''Tell me. Did
Stanley's hand have a short little finger?''

''Not Stanley. He's not part Parker. It's Parker men
that have the short fingers. See Arthur's hand?''

Arthur's palms were pressed against the back window
of the station wagon. The little finger on his right hand
was only half as long as the one on his left hand. The
body in the sawdust shed—the right hand spread. That
was what she had seen. And known. A dwarfed finger
like the one on Jeb Parker's right hand and, as Rosabelle
had just pointed out, like the one on Arthur's hand.

''Dort. Dort, come here,'' Amy called, and Dort came
out from the kitchen. ''I know why that poor baby had
to leave town. I knew I knew something. Oh, that poor
bartered baby.''

Dort stood behind Amy and Rosabelle and looked out
at the two Waldron men as he listened to her explana-

tion. With the Waldrons waiting and leaning against the car, Dort saw the difference between Arthur's right hand and Joe's.

"One more answer," Dort said. "But Arthur will stick to the story he told us—that he believes Stanley killed the Stillman boy. How much will Joe tell us? He's already told a dozen lies."

Rosabelle moved closer to Amy. "Joe wants money. Arthur has money."

Outside, Jones directed the officers. They put Arthur in the sheriff's car and Joe in the state police cruiser and drove out. John Jones headed out, followed by one of his officers driving the station wagon. He had told them he wanted to question Emma Waldron again. Sheriff Woodman was using the phone in Dort's truck.

"How did Joe get here?" Amy asked. "Where's his truck?"

"By the bridge down the road. Where did he appear? Where was he when he struck Chutney?" Dort sat on his heels and ran his fingers over Chut's head and shoulder. "She's got a wicked lump."

"Joe came around from behind the garden shed, below the garage. He was mad and mean. When Chutney dashed at him, he struck the dog in the head, stepped over her where she had fallen and started toward the house," Amy said. "I don't know why he was here, but thinking he was after Rosabelle, I ran to the pond to lead him away."

Rosabelle repeated, "Joe wants money."

Amy took both of Rosabelle's hands and held them as she said, quietly, "But there's no money here. Why did Joe come here?"

Bent Woodman came in and stood quietly beside Dort. He didn't interrupt. Rosabelle looked up at Dort, briefly met Amy's eyes, and then looked down at the floor. "I hide things. Joe thought I hid the money. Thought I gave it to you."

Amy continued to hold Rosabelle's hands and began to rub her thumbs over the joints as they waited for her to continue.

"Arthur gave the money to Stanley. It disappeared. Joe got mad. He said Stanley was keeping all of it. Sometimes he does. He likes to get Joe mad."

Softly and slowly, Amy asked, "When did the money disappear?"

"Friday. Yesterday. The day Stanley goes to Rockland. He gives me pills. He doesn't want me to leave the house." Rosabelle disengaged her hands, reached down into the top of her dress, and handed Dort a roll of bills. "I didn't swallow the pills. I hid the money."

THIRTY-SEVEN

AMY HUGGED Rosabelle and danced her around in a circle. "You're a person, Rosabelle, you're a thinking person. I was afraid you'd been worn down to nothing. Oh, my dear, did I startle you?"

"Yes."

Dort smiled as he watched Amy's show of pleasure and heard Rosabelle's short response. Then he took Rosabelle's hand and led her to the kitchen. Amy and Sheriff Woodman followed and joined them at the table. Maggie settled beside Rosabelle's chair with Chutney on the floor next to Amy. In a low, slow voice, his gentle giant voice, Dort asked Rosabelle how she kept track of the days, how she knew whether it was Tuesday or Friday.

Her thin hands held onto the arms of the chair but, with her eyes on Dort, Rosabelle told him that, after she learned not to swallow the pills Stanley gave her, she looked forward to Fridays. Each week on that day, Stanley went off to Rockland late in the afternoon. And when he left, she knew she had twenty-four hours of freedom. Sometimes he didn't come back until Sunday but it was the hours between Friday afternoon and late Saturday night that she counted as freedom time. She met the dog on a Friday night. That was good. But the dog was lonely and kept coming around every day. Stanley ordered her to keep it away from his house. But how do you make a dog understand that it's only supposed to come on Friday nights?

"But last Saturday Stanley came home early?" Dort kept his voice low.

"He came back in the afternoon. And he was mad. I was in the woods with the dog and that made him madder so he took the dog away. Then Arthur came and they had a fight."

"You told us Arthur brought money last Friday, a week ago," Dort said. "Now you tell us that Arthur came again on Saturday and he and Stanley had a fight. Does Arthur come to your house often?"

"It's Stanley's house," Rosabelle said. "Nothing is mine." Her fingers pleated the edge of the tablecloth as she looked from Dort to the sheriff to Amy. They waited. She turned back to Dort. "Arthur comes every month, once every month. Stanley calls it bank day. He likes it. Arthur doesn't."

Rosabelle told them that last Sunday afternoon Stanley locked her in her room while he and Joe and Arthur talked and argued. When he let her out, after Joe and Arthur left, after dark, she went into the woods, through the trails, trying to find the dog. Stanley came after her. He needed her to cook supper because Arthur had come back and brought the blond boy.

"Did you talk with that boy?" Dort asked.

"He asked me if I could hide the bag he had tossed under the front steps. Told me it was important. Arthur and Stanley were out by Arthur's car, talking. I used the back door, went around, got the bag, and ran down the trail and hid it in the doghouse at Mr. Beaufort's place."

"They didn't see or hear you?" Amy asked.

"No. They kept arguing until Arthur left. After sup-

per, Stanley yelled at me to clean up and to make up a
bed for the boy. Then he locked me in my room.''

"And what happened in the morning?" Dort asked.
"What happened on Monday morning? You told Amy
that Stillman went off with Arthur. Were you still in
your room when Arthur came?''

"Stanley forgot to unlock my door before he went to
work. I listened at the window when Arthur came. He
told the boy he'd take him to meet P. A. Waldron and
find out about his family. Stanley came home early in
the afternoon and he let me out.''

Amy looked at Rosabelle's thin arms and shoulders.
Locked up without food or water. Stanley's cruelty to
his wife, for years, included what he had made Maggie
suffer.

Rosabelle said that when Stanley, Joe, and Arthur
went off together Monday night, Stanley forgot to lock
her in. She wandered through the woods and along the
shore but found no sign of the dog. Stanley didn't come
back until early Tuesday morning. She pretended to be
asleep. After that he was angrier than usual, angry all
the time. And he began hitting her again. Again? Last
year Dr. Hank told Stanley he'd have him put in jail if
he hit Rosabelle again. So he stopped. He just yelled.

Dort asked her what happened on Friday night this
week, what happened yesterday afternoon and evening.

"Stanley told me he was going to Rockland. Said he
was playing Arthur for big money,'' Rosabelle said.
"But after Arthur came and left the money, not the same
as he brought every month, Joe came and he was very
angry. While Joe and Stanley were fighting, I grabbed
the money and ran. But I didn't know where to go, how
to get away. I hid in Beaufort's doghouse all night. No
one found me. After the sun came up, I walked back

through the woods. Stanley wasn't at the house. His truck wasn't there.''

"Did you call anyone?'' Dort asked.

"No. Who would I call? Joe called. He told me Stanley was dead. He said it was my fault and I would go to prison. I locked all the doors and waited for the police. Somebody came but it wasn't a police car. I was afraid to open the door. When Ruth came, I was afraid she'd let Joe get me. I couldn't stop crying. I cried myself sick.''

Amy had made a cup of cocoa and placed it on the table with more strips of buttered bread. Rosabelle sipped and nibbled and looked from Dort to Sheriff Woodman in his brown uniform.

"Thank you, Rosabelle." Dort smiled at her. "You've told us what we need to know today. We'll have more questions, but, in the meantime, you'll be safe here with Amy.''

He turned to Amy. "Maybe you should check the phone messages? Will it help if I start dinner?''

The first voice on the tape was Polly Anderson but, instead of her usual complaints, she told Amy she'd seen a man prowling around between the brook and Amy's garage. Maybe Amy should call the sheriff or that nice Dort Adams. The second message was from Emma Waldron.

Dort and Woodman were as startled as Amy at the venom in the woman's voice as she proclaimed, at length, that Amy Creighton was showing no consideration for Arthur and his wishes. Emma accused Amy of acting as though she was God. Said Amy was destroying the lives of good Christians.

Dort, busy trimming the asparagus, shook the paring knife in Amy's direction and said, "Let's not hear comments about what can or can't happen in Granton. What you've seen and heard today certainly shows you we have a full quota of weird ones on this peninsula, natives and imports.''

Woodman, who had been uncharacteristically quiet throughout the whole afternoon, finished writing in his notebook, slipped it into his pocket, and said, ''Weird and evil and sad. William Stillman was a lost soul from the day Jennie Waldron died and Arthur had to get rid of the evidence of his sin.''

''Move the evidence out of town so he could marry money and indulge his obsession with the Gregg house,'' Dort said.

''That adds to motive. We know now that Arthur brought Stillman to the harbor. In a few hours, with lab reports, we should be able to plug the remaining holes.'' Woodman headed out but paused in the doorway. ''When and how do you suppose Stanley found out about the baby? And where does Joe fit in? There's more than Waldron meanness in this case. Maybe the Still-mans will talk if they're brought back to Granton.''

Amy put the Chinese pork in the oven and set the bulgur wheat to simmer in turkey broth. She brought the jars of applesauce and jam in from the hall where she'd left them while trying to get Emma Waldron out of the house.

''Remember when we didn't have to pause and consider the source when someone used the word *Christian?*'' Amy shook her head. ''Did you think Emma's voice expressed fear as well as anger? I've only heard her talking to others in the grocery store or the post office, but her voice on the phone sounded frantic.''

Chutney asked to be let out. Maggie followed. Rosabelle watched but this time she didn't fuss or moan at the dog's departure. What a change in eight hours.

THIRTY-EIGHT

DR. HANK ARRIVED as they were sitting down to dinner and it didn't take much coaxing to convince him to join them. The doctor told them he'd talked with the state police detectives before Jones went over to question Emma Waldron again. Dort waited until they were having coffee before he asked about Jennie Waldron and the adoption arrangements for her baby. Had he been Jennie's doctor at the time of her death?

"Yes and no. I'd been Jennie's doctor since she broke her leg the summer she was twelve but the year she died my wife and I were in Africa, visiting my brother," Dr. Hank said. "Went over to visit and help him out for several weeks. He ran a children's clinic. Died out there the next year. We came back to Maine in time for Thanksgiving. Jennie's death certificate listed pneumonia as the cause of death. The girl had a predisposition to colds and bronchitis but she was fine when I saw her at the Union Fair in August. Three weeks later, in a warm September, she was dead. Parker Waldron, her father, died the next day. There were rumors of foul play regarding his death but no charges were ever made. The island people had several run-ins with the law that year—alcohol and fishing rights."

"Was Jennie Waldron your patient when she was pregnant?"

"No. That fall, following high school, she went to Portland to take a business course. After the baby was born, she lived with Pauline, her mother. How Jennie loved that child! Pauline told me Arthur arranged the adoption, immediately after Jennie's death, without consulting her. Papers were signed and the baby was out-of-state before Pauline knew what was going on. Woman had just lost her daughter and her husband. She was heartbroken at losing her grandchild. But Pauline was never one to take action about anything. For years she packed clean clothes for Parker every time he went out to Bean Island and when he took his island woman vacationing in Florida."

Dr. Hank turned to Rosabelle, who sat beside him. She hadn't spoken during dinner but appeared to follow the conversation, eyes turned toward whoever was speaking. "I thought in time we might get one or two Waldron wives to stand up for themselves. Ruth's doing better every month. You are, too, aren't you, Rosie?"

"I stopped swallowing the pills," Rosabelle answered. "And I hid the papers and the money."

Dr. Hank looked at Amy, raising his eyebrows. "The papers are the ones the state police detective showed you this afternoon," she said. "When William Stillman headed from Route One toward Granton, he was carrying a canvas bag. Because the bag contained information about his birth parents, according to what Stillman told the man who gave him a ride into Maine and up Route One, the police and sheriff's men searched for them. They couldn't find the bag. Neither could the Waldrons. Joe, Arthur, and Stanley must have been looking everywhere. We now know Stillman asked Rosabelle to hide it and she did."

Amy reached over and placed her hand on Rosabelle's

shoulder. "You snagged that bag out of the doghouse while I was trying to hold Maggie away from the truck wheels, didn't you? And kept it hidden under that big, ugly sweater."

"And the money? What money?" Dr. Hank looked at both women.

Dort answered, "That's not clear yet. Arthur brought cash, four thousand dollars, to Stanley's house and, while Joe and Stan were arguing, Rosabelle snatched the roll of bills and ran off. Hid in the dog house at Beaufort's cottage."

The doctor shook his head. "Waldrons. The meanness goes on. I began stopping and talking with Rosabelle after I found Stanley was physically abusing her. When I discovered the degree of verbal and emotional abuse Rosie's been suffering for years, I wanted to help her feel strong enough to press charges. Opinions by others—even doctors—are not enough to hold up in court. But Rosabelle was too frightened and cowed by Stanley to even sign a complaint."

They drank their coffee in silence, until Dr. Hank added, "The law requires proof. Isn't this murder a case in point? I think you and the police believe Arthur killed William Stillman. But he says Stanley did it. Can anyone prove beyond a reasonable doubt that Arthur Waldron struck that skull-shattering blow? Far easier to picture his surly cousin slamming at someone. Is there any proof that Arthur was near the sawdust shed that night?"

"Stanley had sawdust in his boots," said Rosabelle.

Everyone turned to Rosabelle, still surprised at the information that could tumble from her lips. They hadn't noticed how closely she was following Dr. Hank's words.

"If Arthur had sawdust in his shoes, all traces would

be gone by now. Any sawdust his good wife found in his pockets or shoes would be cleaned away and Emma would have a story ready to cover him,'' Amy said. ''Where was that boy on Monday? Rosabelle saw Stillman leave Stanley's house with Arthur that morning. Where did he eat his last meal of cheese and crackers and milk? Where was that fatal blow struck?''

''Joe hits. When he's mad he tries to hit Stanley,'' Rosabelle said. ''But Stanley's too fast.'' Rosabelle's coffee mug clattered, falling from her hand onto her plate.

''This woman is exhausted,'' Dr. Hank said. ''Curled up in a cold dog house all night. Threatened and dragged all over the place today. She needs a hot bath and bed.''

Dort carried the big chair up to the guest room and Maggie climbed into it while Rosabelle soaked in scented water. Dr. Hank stayed beside her bed until she fell asleep with her fingers twined in the dog's fur.

When the doctor came back down to the kitchen, Amy waved him to the old cushioned Morris chair and he settled back with his hands around the ends of the wide arms, looking weary and old, a frail man showing his eighty-four years.

''Dort, call and find out if Joe and Arthur are being held at the jail,'' he said. ''I've known too many Waldrons. Find out if they're being held or have been released and are free to come back here tonight.''

THIRTY-NINE

"AMY, DO ALL your doors have locks?"

"The doors have locks," Amy answered. "But anyone can smash a window. Do you know something we don't?"

Dr. Hank held up his hand, asking her to wait until Dort finished talking with the sheriff's office.

"Lawyers. More delays." Dort came away from the phone, plopped himself down in the grandfather chair, and looked from Amy to Dr. Hank. "Stillman's lawyer is spouting off again about small town inefficiency. Now Arthur and Emma have a lawyer protecting their rights. Arthur is so sorry his bad cousin killed that boy from Buffalo. Stanley always did have a temper. That lawyer insisted that Joe needed medical attention so he's in the hospital and is threatening to sue because Amy's vicious dog attacked him, chased him into the pond and almost drowned him. That dog is a danger to the town. Must be destroyed."

Amy poured orange juice for each of them and sipped hers as she waited, without comment, for Dort to continue.

"Bent's busy on the phone with New Jersey and New York police. He and Jones are checking on information found in the bag. Some brilliant police officer in Buffalo thinks William Stillman was a disturbed student and made up what we read, wrote out those papers we found. Did it as part of writing stories for English classes. Hogwash. There's no way Stillman or anyone else could have dreamed up the details, facts, and dates about this peninsula and the Waldron family. And there are the newspaper clippings.''

Dr. Hank's hands trembled as he lifted his glass. Dort watched and thought how thin and tired the doctor looked. This morning in the sunlight on Allen's Point Road, Dr. Hank had appeared alert and jovial. Now as he leaned back against the blue-and-white cushion, the doctor looked worn and troubled.

''Several things don't make sense,'' Dort said. ''Amy, you noticed the way some of those papers were written out, with dates. Almost like reports. Was Arthur being blackmailed?''

''Some of those papers were reports,'' Dr. Hank said. He rested his head against the cushion and closed his eyes. ''Doctors carry a lot of secrets. This can be a burden. Through the years I've been guilty of sins of omission—dismissing behavior, bad, unhealthy actions, as the kinds of things Waldrons do. When I was able to do something that would make a difference, I did. But not often enough. I could have done more.''

Amy took the glass of orange juice from his trembling hands and placed it on the stand beside him. ''Thanks, Amy. Too often I didn't have enough facts, enough proof to call in the sheriff.'' The veins in Dr. Hank's hands stood out as he rubbed them down his thighs. ''To protect my conscience and maybe help build up a case, I kept notes, documented records of what I saw and heard. What I suspected. I put in writing what I believed and why.''

The doctor paused and then, eyes still closed, he continued. "I kept my notes. Years of notes. I wanted the facts I had, with the dates, available in writing. Wanted them saved. I came to this peninsula, started doctoring in the county, more than fifty years ago. I've watched Waldron men marry weak women or browbeat their wives into cringing, spiritless creatures. Except Arthur. He never vanquished Emma Ramsdorff. I should have spoken up sooner. I did recognize the name, William Stillman. If I'd never sent those papers, the boy might be alive today."

"Those notes, those records are yours?" Dort asked.

"My notes. My writing. When John Jones showed me those papers, I brought out my old notes. You wondered about the form. That's the way I recorded, documented, what I knew and what I believed but couldn't prove. Jennie told me Arthur was the father of her baby but she didn't want anyone to know. Arthur always wanted his way and his mother encouraged his selfishness. Jennie wanted to protect her son, to give him a chance. Neither of us thought about the baby's short finger, the Parker finger, like Arthur's."

Dort moved over to sit beside Amy and hold her hand as they listened to Dr. Hank fill in the missing parts of the story. He told them that when William Stillman wanted to find his birth parents, neither of his adoptive parents would discuss the matter. A year ago the boy began snooping. In his father's desk he found tax forms done for a Cameron family, big money taxes that included oceanfront property in Maine, taxes for the year William was born. The boy wrote, looking for hospital records in this part of Maine. The old hospital no longer exists but one of the courthouse clerks showed the letter to Dr. Hank.

"I wish I'd let it alone," he said. "But I thought of

Jennie. I wanted to help her son. So, I copied the adoption record and mailed it. That letter led to his death.''

"Many things led to his death,'' Dort said. ''Mailing a record of the adoption was only one. Stillman had started searching and was already focused on this part of Maine. He would have found that record sooner or later. And you know that folks in these parts remember things. Families and babies.''

"Tim Mozeson said the boy told him he had 'stolen' papers from the woman who called herself his mother,'' Amy added.

The phone interrupted. Dort answered and relayed information from the sheriff. Emma had brought a change of clothes to the jail for Arthur and, when he changed, he became so upset Woodman wanted to keep him for more questioning. But their lawyer said there was no cause so Arthur went home with Emma. The Buffalo police reported that one of the college instructors had a story, written by Stillman for an English class, about an adopted child finding his birth parents and going to live on an estate on the coast of Maine. And Stanley Waldron had three bank accounts, each with a balance of thirty thousand dollars.

"It gets crazier and crazier. Everything we learn raises more questions,'' Amy said. ''There's a money element running through all this. How did the Stillmans, who were selling silver and dishes when they left town, get rich—summer camp, prep school rich? In Granton, Maine, where would Stanley Waldron latch on to ninety thousand dollars? I can't think anymore. My mind's shifting into neutral.''

Dort spoke to Dr. Hank. ''If Amy doesn't get to bed, she'll fall asleep and slide off that chair. And you look as though you've had enough for one day.''

The doctor pushed himself up from the Morris chair and held onto one chair arm as he flexed his knees to get them moving. "Dort, stay here tonight with Amy and Rosabelle, will you? This case isn't closed and I won't rest if these women are here alone. Amy said herself that locks on doors don't guarantee safety. I know. You have two dogs here. But someone committed two murders this week and I feel both Amy and Rosabelle are in danger. Dort?"

"I'll stay," Dort answered. "Amy, why don't you go up and wait beside Rosabelle while I give both dogs a run and see Dr. Hank on his way."

Dort's whistle roused Maggie but she wouldn't leave her guard chair until Amy came in. The guestroom, in the front of the house, overlooked the driveway. As Amy slipped into her nightclothes, she saw the doctor's car drive out and watched Dort race the dogs down to the bridge and back. She heard his whistle and, a moment later, Maggie was back in the big chair, her nose on Rosabelle's pillow.

Amy pulled the covers up over Rosabelle's shoulders and turned out the bedside light. "I'll leave her door open and the bathroom light on." Turning to Dort, she said, "Let's go to bed. I'm too tired to think or talk."

Amy was in bed before she realized what she had said. She waited forty seconds before she spoke again to Dort, who was standing in the doorway. "Yes. Come to bed. Come and hold me."

FORTY

CHUTNEY AWAKENED THEM. Not barking but whining and nudging Amy with her nose. Chutney, trained to stay on the floor, had all four feet on the bed as she whined softly but insistently and pushed her nose under Amy's chin. Dort was out of bed in an instant, pulling on his pants. Amy grabbed her robe and followed him into the guestroom where Rosabelle and Maggie huddled together in the middle of the bed, whimpering.

Two flashlight beams moved inside Amy's garage. Dort used a penlight to dial the sheriff and the state police from the phone in Amy's bedroom. Amy knelt beside Rosabelle, rubbed her shoulders, and whispered, "We must be quiet. Mustn't make a sound. Hold onto Maggie."

Dort finished dressing and came back to look down at the driveway. Emma Waldron's station wagon was parked there, headed out. Arthur emerged from Amy's garage carrying a trash bag, full and heavy. As he put the bag into the open rear of the wagon, Emma came out with two more bags. Amy moved over near the window and stood beside Dort where they could watch the Waldrons carrying the bags of sawdust from her car to the station wagon.

"What on earth?" Amy whispered. "Where's your truck?"

"Bent took it."

With no vehicle in the driveway, Arthur and Emma had no reason to believe anyone was in the house except Amy and Rosabelle. Although both of them knew about the two dogs, they didn't seem worried. Were they prepared to shoot? Dort and Amy watched Arthur and Emma continue to move the bags of sawdust from Amy's car to Emma's wagon. Had they taken all the bags she had left in the hatchback? Without turning on the headlights, they started the car and drove out of the curving driveway.

Dort shouted, "Success! They did it," and danced Amy around the room. Both dogs barked. Rosabelle moved from the bed to the other front window. Flashing lights swept along the town road. Arthur and Emma's quiet exit had run into the sheriff's patrol and the state police, blocking Amy's lane. How would those two explain stealing bags of sawdust, in the middle of the night, taking them from Amy's car in her garage?

"Turn the outside lights on so the officers will know you're OK," Dort said. "But don't let the dogs out. Emma and Arthur came prepared to deal with the dogs, somehow."

Amy took Rosabelle into her bedroom, opened dresser drawers and the sliding doors of the closet and said, "Choose. We need to dress before the sheriff comes. I'll be right back."

Downstairs, Amy moved from the front door to the kitchen door and out into her office, switching on all the outside lights, flooding the lawns beyond each door and the driveway beside the garage. Chutney punctuated her growls with low barks as she watched the driveway with her paws on the sill of a living room window.

Dort took the kitchen flashlight and a plastic bag and

picked up a trowel on the back steps. Chunks of raw beef were spread out beyond the entry. Matt Torrey, one of Bent's tall deputies, joined him and held the flashlight while Dort scooped up the bloody beef.

"Woodman and Jones want to question the Waldrons and they'd like to do it here, now, if Mrs. Creighton would let them bring the two into her house," Matt said.

Dort handed the bag and scoop to Torrey, told him to check in front of the other doors, then stomped across the porch and into the kitchen. Amy took a look at his face and hands, turned on the faucet, and sprayed his hands with liquid cleanser.

"Poisoned meat?"

"Pounds of it."

She handed him a towel. "And now?"

"Bent wants to bring them in here for questioning."

"I don't want either of them in my house," Amy said. "But it will save time. Maybe if they're questioned now when they've just been caught doing something stupid, we'll find some missing pieces. I'm tired. Tell him yes."

Rosabelle and Maggie stood in the kitchen doorway, the large black dog beside a slender woman wearing tattersall slacks and a red sweatshirt. But it wasn't just attractive clothes and color that made Rosabelle appear more alert. In place of the cringing posture, she stood in her bare feet, head up and shoulders back, listening and waiting.

"I promised you I would not let Arthur in this house," Amy said. "But the police need to question both Arthur and Emma. They're bringing them in here to do that. You may stay down here with Dort and with me or you and Maggie can wait upstairs. I'm going up to get dressed. Dort, will you light the fire and turn on the lights in the living room?"

The fireplace draft was good. The second logs were catching when John Jones, Bent Woodman, and their men brought the Waldrons into the living room. At Jones's request, the officers moved the two big old Hilton wing chairs and asked Arthur to sit in the one placed directly behind the one in which they had seated Emma. This way, neither could watch the other one's facial expressions. Emma's bulk more than filled the front chair and the voluminous fabric of her mauve corduroy garment spread over the upholstered arms of the chair. Arthur, in his usual blue-gray business suit, appeared diminished in the matching chair.

Amy stood in the double doorway with Dort behind her and Chutney, growling deep in her throat, close beside her knee. Dort leaned down and whispered, "Wouldn't you like a photo of those two pillars of the church as they are now in those chairs?"

When the recording machine had been set up and tested, Jones and Woodman read Emma and Arthur their rights and this time they didn't immediately demand their lawyer. The officers coordinated their questioning, going from Arthur to Emma and from one subject to another. Amy listened with increasing respect for the skills of the two men and admiration for how well they balanced and supported each other. Both the sheriff and the detective moved back and forth over the week's events, questioning without pausing after the answers, catching discrepancies and lies.

This morning Arthur told the sheriff he had been working in his office Friday night but there had been no lights there. In answering the phone and in talking with Detective Jones, Emma had repeatedly stated that Arthur had not been at home Friday night. Where was he during those hours when Stanley was killed? Why did Arthur give Stanley $4,000 in cash yesterday afternoon? How much of that money was supposed to be passed on to Joe? Payment for what? The source of the money?

Repeatedly, the men asked why were Emma and Arthur stealing sawdust out of Mrs. Creighton's car, from her private garage, in the middle of the night? And before they could answer, immediately asked another question: Where was William Stillman, Arthur's son, killed? How long had Emma known that Arthur and his sister were the parents of the murdered boy? Why were Waldrons up at the Fullerton farm on Monday night? Did Emma help lift Stillman's dead body into the sawdust shed?

Arthur and Emma had come into Amy's living room with their usual pretentious, head-high arrogance—what Amy called their "let's humor the peasants" manner. But after five minutes of being questioned, neither Arthur nor Emma was able to think fast enough to fabricate matching falsehoods. Both resorted to muttering that they didn't know, had no answers to the officer's questions.

John Jones lowered his voice and slowed the tempo of his questioning. "Let's go back to the immediate question. Why were you stealing sawdust from Mrs. Creighton's car in her garage, at two-thirty a.m.?"

The logs in the fireplace crackled. Chutney growled softly. John Jones looked from Arthur to Emma and waited. Emma tried to turn around but the officers on each side of her leaned in close to the high wings of the chair. No one spoke.

Amy and Chutney turned in response to a movement. Rosabelle and Maggie came into the doorway, quietly, and stood beside Amy. Rosabelle's face wore a blank expression but she looked across the room at Arthur with an unflinching stare.

Arthur started to rise. "Get that woman out of here. She's crazy. She needs to be locked up. Get her out of here."

The sheriff's deputies pushed Arthur back into the chair. John Jones repeated his question and added, "You're both under arrest for trespassing and theft."

"You don't arrest people for taking a few bags of sawdust," Emma said. "Sawdust is free."

Still using a low, slow voice, Jones asked, "Why did you drive here in the middle of the night to steal free sawdust from inside Amy Creighton's car, inside her garage?"

Rosabelle continued to stare at Arthur and asked, "Why are you here in the middle of the night?"

Amy leaned back against Dort. His large hands rested gently on her shoulders. The scene in her living room took on a new dimension in her mind—swirling into a spooky, unreal vision from a scary childhood story—unrelenting underworld dwarfs encircling and creeping closer and closer to the captured enemy, waiting for them to scream and give up.

A knock on the front door broke the tension. Dort answered and brought Ruth Waldron and her two boys down the wide hallway to the living room entrance. "I need to know what's going on," she said. "The hospital called. Joe walked out two hours ago. Arthur Waldron, I want you to tell me why you were going to give money to my husband. For what? What were you paying Stanley for? Where were you getting all the money?"

Once again, Emma tried to turn to look at Arthur. Once again the officers closed in on each side. Her voice trembled. With anger? "Arthur, what money is Ruth talking about? How much?"

Arthur kept his eyes on the back of the chair in which Emma was sitting and said, "Money is personal, a private matter. Emma, this is not a time to speak of money. We do not discuss money with strangers." Arthur's voice, despite the circumstances, had the same monotone blandness as the voice in which he had spoken to Amy that morning, yesterday morning, at Stanley's house.

But Emma repeated her question, "Arthur, what money is Ruth talking about?"

Dort interrupted, as though an idea had suddenly come to him. "Stanley Waldron's bank accounts total more than ninety thousand dollars. If Arthur paid Stan ten thousand a year during the past nine years…"

Ruth gasped. Emma cried out. What began as deep, guttural gulpings rose to piercing screams that sounded like the amplified cries of six wounded porcupines before she shrieked, "You lied. Arthur Waldron, you lied to me. Lied, lied, lied. I'll kill you the way I killed your bastard son!"

FORTY-ONE

ARTHUR CRINGED, shrinking back into his chair. Jones and Woodman helped police officers hold Emma in the other. The woman vibrated with wrath and continued to make shrill, venomous threats. Rosabelle and Ruth's boys retreated to the hall to escape Emma's loud, vitriolic voice. Maggie stood guard in front of them until Amy asked Ruth to take the three upstairs. Dort, the largest man present, walked over and stood in front of Emma.

The woman quieted and silence held until she said, "I want my lawyer. I want to call my lawyer."

Bentley Woodman, looking exhausted and irritated, said, "You may call your lawyer. You may call sixteen lawyers and pay them with your money or Arthur's money. But I still want to know what you're doing here in the middle of the night."

Amy spoke from the doorway. "What did you lose in the sawdust the night you dumped William Stillman's body in that shed?"

"I never dumped that boy in that shed," Emma spat out. "I want my lawyer."

John Jones signaled to his officers and they stood by with handcuffs ready as Jones and Dort helped Emma up out of the chair. "You may call from the jail," Jones said and before Emma could lunge her bulk at him, her wrists were cuffed behind her back.

Dort backed the Waldron's station wagon down beyond the garage, leaving the driveway free for the sheriff's men and the state police to bring in their cars and turn around. Arthur and Emma were led out, settled into separate vehicles, and taken off to jail. Amy joined Dort for another check around each doorway, looking for any missed chunks of doped or poisoned meat.

Once again Amy Creighton's back yard was silent but the invasion of the prowler Friday night and the Waldrons tonight had shattered the feeling of pleasure and comfort the darkness usually brought to her. Amy swung her flashlight beam around the front steps for a final check before calling the dogs out.

She could hear the voices of Ruth's boys from the open windows upstairs in the guestroom. Dort came up beside her as the older boy said, "Dad told us Arthur was a smart investor. He was good with money but wouldn't help any other Waldrons make money. Dad didn't like Arthur much."

The younger boy added, "And he always got someone else to do his dirty work and he didn't like to pay. Then Stanley got mean again and stole the money Dad needs to pay for his new truck."

Ruth's voice had a weary tone. "Your father seems to have told you more about Arthur and his money than he told me. Tell me about this dirty work. Is that why your father wanted a new truck? To haul manure for Emma's shrubs?"

"Mom, you're being silly. You know Dad doesn't want his truck to get messed up. He keeps washing it. You know that."

"I'm too tired to think. Tell me about Arthur's dirty work."

Both boys were silent. It was Rosabelle who answered. "Arthur sold more insurance after there was damage. Stanley took Joe to help him."

Dort whispered to Amy, "Windows broken in summer cottages. Car windshields smashed. Holes in sailboats. We've been on this for months. Waldrons!"

Amy pointed to the station wagon. "Let's check out my guess that someone lost something in the sawdust. We can dump the bags out, one at a time, under this garage spotlight."

The rear of the station wagon held six bags. Amy stepped into her garage with her flashlight and called out, "The seventh, the last one I filled, is in here. I removed it so I could see out the back window."

Ruth called from the guestroom window, "Can we help?"

She and Rosabelle and the boys came down and stood on the far side of the tarpaulin Dort spread out on the driveway, under the floodlight. Rosabelle, in her bare feet, looked like a child as she stood with Ruth's boys.

Amy knelt with her back to the garage to avoid shadows and Dort slowly emptied the sawdust from the seventh bag. "Stop!" Amy's voice broke the silence as light reflected from an object spilled from the bag. Dort and Amy spread their fingers through the soft wood particles.

"There," said Amy in a whisper.

Dort reached down and picked up Arthur's tie clip, his prized award from the congregation of his church. Arthur Waldron had been in the Morse Mill shed the night his son's body was dumped there.

Without looking at it, Ruth recited the citation engraved on the back: "Arthur Waldron—A Number One Christian."

Dort looked at Amy. "When Emma brought fresh clothes to Arthur at the jail, was it then he noticed his tie clip was missing? Does that explain why they came here tonight?"

They turned back to the house and followed the dogs inside. When the kitchen phone rang, Dort answered. Sheriff Woodman wanted them to know Joe Waldron had been picked up on Route One. He was in jail, charged with assault, vandalism, withholding evidence, and resisting arrest. Dort asked the sheriff to tell Jones they now knew why Arthur and Emma had come to steal the bags of sawdust. He'd deliver the small bit of physical evidence later. After daylight.

FORTY-TWO

AMY CREIGHTON mulched her strawberries early Monday morning. The dew on the plants sparkled in the long rays of the rising sun. Her plastic dustpan served well as a tool to dump the fresh-scented wood bits as Amy lifted the burgeoning leaves to slip sawdust between the plants. She wielded the clippers she carried in the back pocket of her jeans to snip off crowded plants and to sever the runners between mother and daughter plants.

Maggie and Chutney had come back from the pond, wet and panting, and flopped down on the lawn nearby. Joe Waldron's footprints along the upper edge of the strawberry bed showed the way he had come from the woods and around the garage on Saturday. Joe was still in jail. Ruth found the cash Joe had borrowed from Mel Driscoll to make a truck payment with and Dort returned it to the old man. Joe had no other money for a truck payment. No money for bail.

Dr. Hank had said Rosabelle could go back to Allen's Point today, if she wanted to, if she thought she'd feel comfortable there with Maggie. Dort and Ruth had helped her arrange a graveside service for Stanley to be held on Tuesday. Beaufort had asked his mother to let him return to the city.

Amy spread the sawdust from the last three bags over folded newspapers to make a weed-free picking path

through the middle of the strawberry patch. The spring
chore she had set out to do last Wednesday was now
completed. Many lives had changed in the five days
since she had gone into that mill shed and filled seven
bags, lowering the high pile until, without being aware
of it, she scraped up Arthur's tie pin, until the sliding
wood bits revealed the boy's body.

In the sawdust dumped from that seventh bag, Amy
had found two crumpled candy wrappers, the same brand
as the one Tim had seen tucked among the rocks at
Beaufort's place, the kind of bar he had given William
Stillman on that rainy May night. Rosabelle said Arthur
left candy wrappers in the dooryard every time he came
to the Allen's Point house. Apparently he had dropped
these while he was discarding his son's body.

The Maine Sunday newspapers featured articles on the
Granton murders. Reporters wrote stories based on facts
found in the files, retelling past news—the butchering of
the Fullertons' prize steers and the capture and arrest of
teenager Stanley Waldron, who had been hiding out in
the same sawdust shed where Stillman's body had been
found, an irony not lost on the reporters. Local and state
journalists would ferret out and play up more angles now
that Arthur, Emma, and Joe had been arrested. One paper
had revisited questions about foul play raised when the
body of Arthur's father had been found on Bean Island.
They'd probably write about Jennie and the double funeral next.

Some diligent reporter would search and find that, two
weeks after his marriage to Emma Ramsdorff, Arthur
Waldron opened an account in a Boston bank by depos-
iting a check from his father-in-law for one hundred
thousand dollars. In the county probate records, reporters
could read old Kurt Ramsdorff's will. As long as Arthur

remained married to Emma, he didn't have to worry
about money. Her annual income from the trust set up
by her father was ninety thousand dollars. In Granton,
Maine, that was big money.

Reports of vandalism on the peninsula's cars, cottages, and boats would be reviewed. Some papers would
publish interviews with owners of summer cottages and
question the insurance Arthur Waldron sold them after
shore property "accidents" and wanton destruction.
Was Arthur's need to be in control of something so
strong that he needed to play that dangerous game? Neither he nor Emma lacked for income. Was it a need to
control that explained his paying Stanley for years not
to tell about the baby, the son he had paid the Stillmans
to take away? Money and power. Joe told the homicide
detective he and Stanley had gone to Arthur's house for
a showdown, Stanley in his muddy boots. Said Emma
struck Stanley with an iron skillet while the four of them
argued in the kitchen of the Gregg house. Why did they
move him to the Bellhouse driveway? There were many
questions still to be answered.

The Gregg house would make good copy with photos
of how it looked before Arthur bought it in 1979, and
how it looked today. Captain Ruel Gregg was an important figure in local maritime history and the colonial
style house he had built in 1805 was probably the oldest
house still intact between Route One and Sacaja Harbor.
In the past ten years, several national magazines had
featured the house with descriptions and photographs of
the extensive, authentic restoration of this historic land-
mark. With quotes from Arthur and Emma on their years
of devoted labor.

Among the papers in William Stillman's bag was a
list of securities that matched the ones Courtney Cam-

eron's heirs had reported missing. Just a list but it suggested a possible base of the Stillman wealth. Cameron's death occurred shortly before their hasty departure from Maine.

Amy was not really pleased to find that her premise proved to be true. There was a thread of greed and money woven through all the events. But fully as strong was Emma's fear of losing her husband, her house, and her status in the community as a married woman. She needed those. The discomfort and loneliness her hulking size had forced upon her since earliest childhood had been held at bay while she had a husband and, through marriage, a place in the church community and the absorbing work of restoring and showing the Gregg house.

Emma loved that house, loved planning restoration work and going forth, seeking the right furnishings, the right materials. She thoroughly enjoyed being the owner and hostess when historical societies came to view the Gregg house. Emma had always known that Arthur's obsession for the house led him to marrying her. She knew it was their mutual pleasure in the house that kept them together. But Emma had lived in that elegant old colonial with fear. Poor William Stillman, searching for a family, had his last meal in the beautiful home of P. A. Waldron. Crackers and cheese. Arthur's son, once again unwanted, an embarrassing impediment, and Arthur's cousin Stanley fell under Emma's anger born of fear. She struck to protect and hold on to what she needed.

Amy was putting her tools back into the garden shed when the dogs announced Dort's arrival. A new day, warm May sunshine and three Waldrons in custody. As Amy Creighton moved into Dort Adam's embrace, she thought of that October painting. Perhaps Lou Fullerton would sell it.

SCAVENGERS

A Posadas County Mystery

Steven F. Havill

A man's body is found in the
unforgiving New Mexico desert,
the beginning of a brutal murder
spree that has roots on both
sides of the border.

Retired sheriff Bill Gastner
offers unerring logic and
horse sense to new undersheriff
Estelle Reyes-Guzman in her
attempts to identify the "Juan" Doe.
When another body turns up in a
shallow grave and a suspicious fire
takes a third life, the terrible twist
finally offers the break Estelle has
been looking for, one that will lead
her back into a harsh, merciless
desert where death welcomes all.

"...there's solid pleasure to be derived
from Havill's consistently good writing,
colorful cast, and dead-on sense of place."
—*Kirkus Reviews*

Available February 2004 at your favorite retail outlet.

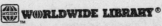
WSFH482

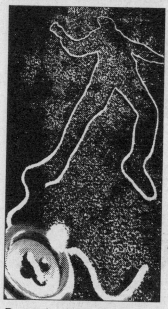

BUTTONS & FOES

A MANDY DYER MYSTERY

Dolores Johnson

Denver dry cleaner Mandy Dyer is shocked to learn that a favorite customer has died and left Mandy something—two trash bags packed with worthless old clothing. Full of questions, Mandy notices some antique buttons sewn onto the dresses and suspects the woman was trying to send her a message.

Convinced the button mystery is linked to her friend's sudden demise, Mandy starts nosing around the local button-collecting clubs...and stumbles onto another murder. And while removing bloodstains may be a cinch for an expert dry cleaner, Mandy hopes she won't have to try her luck against a cold-blooded killer.

"...entertaining, amusing amateur sleuth."
—Harriet Klausner

Available March 2004.

WDJ487

THE FUGITIVE KING

SARAH R. SHABER

A PROFESSOR SIMON SHAW MYSTERY

When the remains of a young woman who disappeared forty years ago are found in North Carolina, the man who went to prison for her murder wants history professor Simon Shaw to prove that he didn't kill her.

Putting small-town gossip, obliging relatives and old memories to good use, Shaw investigates. But what would drive a man to confess to a murder he didn't commit? A second murder disguised as an accident points Shaw in the right direction, leading him to a stunning discovery hidden deep in the hills, to a secret worth lying—and killing—for.

"An engaging mystery in a too-little-known series."
—Booklist

Available March 2004 at your favorite retail outlet.

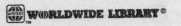

WSRS485

COLD COMFORT
Scott Mackay

A Detective Barry Gilbert Mystery

When the stepdaughter of a prominent politician is found frozen with a bullet through her heart, overworked, underpaid homicide detective Barry Gilbert inherits the case.

The bizarre nature of the crime doesn't bode well for a quick and tidy solution. The victim's apartment was trashed and the intruder killed her parrot. She was never seen leaving her building on the security videotape. Add a large sum of stolen money and a dead sister and Gilbert is tackling a crime filled with dark secrets, dangerous relations and a killer convinced he can get away with murder.

"The twists and turns...recall the work of procedural master Hillary Waugh."
—*Ellery Queen Mystery Magazine*

Available March 2004.

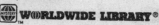

UP
AND
DOWN

AN INSPECTOR DON PACKHAM MYSTERY

Mat Coward

A man is found pitchforked to death in his garden, and Constable Frank Mitchell finds himself paired with the legendary Inspector Don Packham. Unfortunately, Mitchell is never sure whether he'll be working with the upbeat, jovial Packham or his manic-depressive alter ego.

Why would anyone murder an old man who did little but tend his beans? The answer, Packham is certain, lies with the other gardeners in the allotment where the victim toiled daily. Digging into the lives of the other "plotters," the two uncover the real dirt surrounding a garden-variety killer.

"...impressive...will remind readers of long-suffering Lewis and moody Morse in the Colin Dexter series."
—*Booklist*

Available February 2004 at your favorite retail outlet.

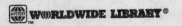

WORLDWIDE LIBRARY®

WMC484